The Ladybird;
The Fox

D. H. Lawrence

The Ladybird; The Fox

Copyright © 2018 Indo-European Publishing

The present edition is a reproduction of previous publication of this work. Minor typographical errors may have been corrected without note, however, for an authentic reading experience the spelling, punctuation, and capitalization have been retained from the original text.

ISBN: 978-1-60444-846-7

CONTENTS

The Ladybird

How many swords had Lady Beveridge in her pierced heart! Yet there always seemed room for another. Since she had determined that her heart of pity and kindness should never die. If it had not been for this determination she herself might have died of sheer agony, in the years 1916 and 1917, when her boys were killed, and her brother, and death seemed to be mowing with wide swaths through her family. But let us forget.

Lady Beveridge loved humanity, and come what might, she would continue to love it. Nay, in the human sense, she would love her enemies. Not the criminals among the enemy, the men who committed atrocities. But the men who were enemies through no choice of their own. She would be swept into no general hate.

Somebody had called her the soul of England. It was not ill said, though she was half Irish. But of an old, aristocratic, loyal family famous for its brilliant men. And she, Lady Beveridge, had for years as much influence on the tone of English politics as any individual alive. The close friend of the real leaders in the House of Lords and in the Cabinet, she was content that the men should act, so long as they breathed from her as from the rose of life the pure fragrance of truth and genuine love. She had no misgiving regarding her own spirit.

She, she would never lower her delicate silken flag. For instance, throughout all the agony of the war she never forgot the enemy prisoners; she was determined to do her best for them. During the first years she still had influence. But during the last years of the war power slipped out of the hands of her and her sort, and she found she could do nothing any more: almost nothing. Then it seemed as if the many swords had gone home into the heart of this little, unyielding Mater Dolorosa. The new generation jeered at her. She was a shabby, old-fashioned little aristocrat, and her drawing-room was out of date.

But we anticipate. The years 1916 and 1917 were the years when the old spirit died for ever in England. But Lady Beveridge struggled on. She was being beaten.

It was in the winter of 1917 — or in the late autumn. She had been for a fortnight sick, stricken, paralysed by the fearful death of her youngest boy. She felt she MUST give in, and just die. And then she remembered how many others were lying in agony.

So she rose, trembling, frail, to pay a visit to the hospital where lay the enemy sick and wounded, near London. Countess Beveridge was still a privileged woman. Society was beginning to jeer at this little, worn bird of an out-of-date righteousness and aesthetic. But they dared not think ill of her.

She ordered the car and went alone. The Earl, her husband, had taken his gloom to Scotland. So, on a sunny, wan November morning Lady Beveridge descended at the hospital, Hurst Place. The guard knew her, and saluted as she passed. Ah, she was used to such deep respect! It was strange that she felt it so bitterly, when the respect became shallower. But she did. It was the beginning of the end to her.

The matron went with her into the ward. Alas, the beds were all full, and men were even lying on pallets on the floor. There was a desperate, crowded dreariness and helplessness in the place: as if nobody wanted to make a sound or utter a word. Many of the men were haggard and unshaven, one was delirious, and talking fitfully in the Saxon dialect. It went to Lady Beveridge's heart. She had been educated in Dresden, and had had many dear friendships in the city. Her children also had been educated there. She heard the Saxon dialect with pain.

She was a little, frail, bird-like woman, elegant, but with that touch of the blue-stocking of the nineties which was unmistakable. She fluttered delicately from bed to bed, speaking in perfect German, but with a thin, English intonation: and always asking if there was anything she could do. The men were mostly officers and gentlemen. They made little requests which she wrote down in a book. Her long, pale, rather worn face, and her nervous little gestures somehow inspired confidence.

One man lay quite still, with his eyes shut. He had a black beard. His face was rather small and sallow. He might be dead. Lady Beveridge looked at him earnestly, and fear came into her face.

'Why, Count Dionys!' she said, fluttered. 'Are you asleep?'

It was Count Johann Dionys Psanek, a Bohemian. She had known him when he was a boy, and only in the spring of 1914 he and his wife had stayed with Lady Beveridge in her country house in Leicestershire.

His black eyes opened: large, black, unseeing eyes, with curved black lashes. He was a small man, small as a boy, and his face too was rather small. But all the lines were fine, as if they had been fired with a keen male energy. Now the yellowish swarthy paste of his flesh seemed dead, and the fine black brows seemed drawn on the face of one dead. The eyes, however, were alive: but only just alive, unseeing and unknowing.

'You know me, Count Dionys? You know me, don't you?' said Lady Beveridge, bending forward over the bed.

There was no reply for some time. Then the black eyes gathered a look of recognition, and there came the ghost of a polite smile.

'Lady Beveridge.' The lips formed the words. There was practically no sound.

'I am so glad you can recognize me. And I am so sorry you are hurt. I am so sorry.'

The black eyes watched her from that terrible remoteness of death, without changing.

'There is nothing I can do for you? Nothing at all?' she said, always speaking German.

And after a time, and from a distance, came the answer from his eyes, a look of weariness, of refusal, and a wish to be left alone; he was unable to strain himself into consciousness. His eyelids dropped.

'I am so sorry,' she said. 'If ever there is anything I can do — '

The eyes opened again, looking at her. He seemed at last to hear, and it was as if his eyes made the last weary gesture of a polite bow. Then slowly his eyelids closed again.

Poor Lady Beveridge felt another sword-thrust of sorrow in her heart, as she stood looking down at the motionless face, and at the black fine beard. The black hairs came out of his skin thin and fine, not very close together. A queer, dark, aboriginal little face he had, with a fine little nose: not an Aryan, surely. And he was going to die.

He had a bullet through the upper part of his chest, and another bullet had broken one of his ribs. He had been in hospital five days.

Lady Beveridge asked the matron to ring her up if anything happened. Then she drove away, saddened. Instead of going to Beveridge House, she went to her daughter's flat near the park — near Hyde Park. Lady Daphne was poor. She had married a commoner, son of one of the most famous politicians in England, but a man with no money. And Earl Beveridge had wasted most of the large fortune that had come to him, so that the daughter had very little, comparatively.

Lady Beveridge suffered, going in the narrow doorway into the rather ugly flat. Lady Daphne was sitting by the electric fire in the small yellow drawing-room, talking to a visitor. She rose at once, seeing her little mother.

'Why, mother, ought you to be out? I'm sure not.'

'Yes, Daphne darling. Of course I ought to be out.'

'How are you?' The daughter's voice was slow and sonorous, protective, sad. Lady Daphne was tall, only twenty-five years old. She had been one of the beauties, when the war broke out, and her father had hoped she would make a splendid match. Truly, she had married fame: but without money. Now, sorrow, pain, thwarted passion had done her great damage. Her husband was missing in the East. Her baby had been born dead. Her two darling brothers were dead. And she was ill, always ill.

A tall, beautifully-built girl, she had the fine stature of her father. Her shoulders were still straight. But how thin her white throat! She wore a simple black frock stitched with coloured wool round the top, and held in a loose coloured girdle: otherwise no ornaments. And her face was lovely, fair, with a soft exotic white complexion and delicate pink cheeks. Her hair was soft and heavy, of a lovely pallid gold colour, ash-blond. Her hair, her complexion were so perfectly cared for as to be almost artificial, like a hot-house flower.

But alas, her beauty was a failure. She was threatened with phthisis, and was far too thin. Her eyes were the saddest part of her. They had slightly reddened rims, nerve-worn, with heavy, veined lids that seemed as if they did not want to keep up. The eyes themselves were large and of a beautiful green-blue colour. But they were full, languid, almost glaucous.

Standing as she was, a tall, finely-built girl, looking down with affectionate care on her mother, she filled the heart with ashes. The little pathetic mother, so wonderful in her way, was not really to be pitied for all her sorrow. Her life was in her sorrows, and her efforts on behalf of the sorrows of others. But Daphne was not born for grief and philanthropy. With her splendid frame, and her lovely, long, strong legs, she was Artemis or Atalanta rather than Daphne. There was a certain width of brow and even of chin that spoke a strong, reckless nature, and the curious, distraught slant of her eyes told of a wild energy dammed up inside her.

That was what ailed her: her own wild energy. She had it from her father, and from her father's desperate race. The earldom had begun with a riotous, dare-devil border soldier, and this was the blood that flowed on. And alas, what was to be done with it?

Daphne had married an adorable husband: truly an adorable husband. Whereas she needed a dare-devil. But in her MIND she hated all dare-devils: she had been brought up by her mother to admire only the good.

So, her reckless, anti-philanthropic passion could find no outlet — and SHOULD find no outlet, she thought. So her own blood turned against her, beat on her own nerves, and destroyed her. It was nothing but frustration and anger which made her ill, and made the doctors fear consumption. There it was, drawn on her rather wide mouth: frustration, anger, bitterness. There it was the same in the roll of her green-blue eyes, a slanting, averted look: the same anger furtively turning back on itself. This anger reddened her eyes and shattered her nerves. And yet her whole will was fixed in her adoption of her mother's creed, and in condemnation of her handsome, proud, brutal father, who had made so much misery in the family. Yes, her will was fixed in the determination that life should be gentle and good and benevolent. Whereas her blood was reckless, the blood of daredevils. Her will was the stronger of the two. But her blood had its revenge on her. So it is with strong natures today: shattered from the inside.

'You have no news, darling?' asked the mother.

'No. My father-in-law had information that British prisoners had been brought into Hasrun, and that details would be forwarded by the Turks. And there was a rumour from some Arab prisoners that Basil was one of the British brought in wounded.'

'When did you hear this?'

'Primrose came in this morning.'

'Then we can hope, dear.'

'Yes.'

Never was anything more dull and bitter than Daphne's affirmative of hope. Hope had become almost a curse to her. She wished there need be no such thing. Ha, the torment of hoping, and the INSULT to one's soul. Like the importunate widow dunning for her deserts. Why could it not all be just clean disaster, and have done with it? This dilly-dallying with despair was worse than despair. She had hoped so much: ah, for her darling brothers she had hoped with such anguish. And the two she loved best were dead. So were most others she had hoped for, dead. Only this uncertainty about her husband still rankling.

'You feel better, dear?' said the little, unquenched mother.

'Rather better,' came the resentful answer.

'And your night?'

'No better.'

There was a pause.

'You are coming to lunch with me, Daphne darling?'

'No, mother dear. I promised to lunch at the Howards with Primrose. But I needn't go for a quarter of an hour. Do sit down.'

Both women seated themselves near the electric fire. There was that bitter pause, neither knowing what to say. Then Daphne roused herself to look at her mother.

'Are you sure you were fit to go out?' she said. 'What took you out so suddenly?'

'I went to Hurst Place, dear. I had the men on my mind, after the way the newspapers had been talking.'

'Why ever do you read the newspapers!' blurted Daphne, with a certain burning, acid anger. 'Well,' she said, more composed. 'And do you feel better now you've been?'

'So many people suffer besides ourselves, darling.'

'I know they do. Makes it all the worse. It wouldn't matter if it were only just us. At least, it would matter, but one could bear it more easily. To be just one of a crowd all in the same state.'

'And some even worse, dear.'

'Oh, quite! And the worse it is for all, the worse it is for one.'

'Is that so, darling? Try not to see too darkly. I feel if I can give just a little bit of myself to help the others — you know — it alleviates me. I feel that what I can give to the men lying there, Daphne, I give to my own boys. I can only help them now through helping others. But I can still do that, Daphne, my girl.'

6

And the mother put her little white hand into the long, white cold hand of her daughter. Tears came to Daphne's eyes, and a fearful stony grimace to her mouth.

'It's so wonderful of you that you can feel like that,' she said.

'But you feel the same, my love. I know you do.'

'No, I don't. Everyone I see suffering these same awful things, it makes me wish more for the end of the world. And I quite see that the world won't end — '

'But it will get better, dear. This time it's like a great sickness — like a terrible pneumonia tearing the breast of the world.'

'Do you believe it will get better? I don't.'

'It will get better. Of course it will get better. It is perverse to think otherwise, Daphne. Remember what HAS been before, even in Europe. Ah, Daphne, we must take a bigger view.'

'Yes, I suppose we must.'

The daughter spoke rapidly, from the lips, in a resonant, monotonous tone. The mother spoke from the heart.

'And Daphne, I found an old friend among the men at Hurst Place.'

'Who?'

'Little Count Dionys. You remember him?'

'Quite. What's wrong?'

'Wounded rather badly — through the chest. So ill.'

'Did you speak to him?'

'Yes. I recognized him in spite of his beard.'

'Beard!'

'Yes — a black beard. I suppose he could not be shaven. It seems strange that he is still alive, poor man.'

'Why strange? He isn't old. How old is he?'

'Between thirty and forty. But so ill, so wounded, Daphne. And so small. So small, so sallow — smorto, you know the Italian word. The way dark people look. There is something so distressing in it.'

'Does he look VERY small now — uncanny?' asked the daughter.

'No, not uncanny. Something of the terrible far-awayness of a child that is very ill and can't tell you what hurts it. Poor Count Dionys, Daphne. I didn't know, dear, that his eyes were so black, and his lashes so curved and long. I had never thought of him as beautiful.'

'Nor I. Only a little comical. Such a dapper little man.'

'Yes. And yet now, Daphne, there is something remote and in a sad way heroic in his dark face. Something primitive.'

'What did he say to you?'

'He couldn't speak to me. Only with his lips, just my name.'

'So bad as that?'

'Oh yes. They are afraid he will die.'

'Poor Count Dionys. I liked him. He was a bit like a monkey, but he had his points. He gave me a thimble on my seventeenth birthday. Such an amusing thimble.'

'I remember, dear.'

'Unpleasant wife, though. Wonder if he minds dying far away from her. Wonder if she knows.'

'I think not. They didn't even know his name properly. Only that he was a colonel of such and such a regiment.'

'Fourth Cavalry,' said Daphne. 'Poor Count Dionys. Such a lovely name, I always thought: Count Johann Dionys Psanek. Extraordinary dandy he was. And an amazingly good dancer, small, yet electric. Wonder if he minds dying.'

'He was so full of life, in his own little animal way. They say small people are always conceited. But he doesn't look conceited now, dear. Something ages old in his face — and, yes, a certain beauty, Daphne.'

'You mean long lashes.'

'No. So still, so solitary — and ages old, in his race. I suppose he must belong to one of those curious little aboriginal races of Central Europe. I felt quite new beside him.'

'How nice of you,' said Daphne.

Nevertheless, next day Daphne telephoned to Hurst Place to ask for news of him. He was about the same. She telephoned every day. Then she was told he was a little stronger. The day she received the message that her husband was wounded and a prisoner in Turkey, and that his wounds were healing, she forgot to telephone for news of the little enemy Count. And the following day she telephoned that she was coming to the hospital to see him.

He was awake, more restless, more in physical excitement. They could see the nausea of pain round his nose. His face seemed to Daphne curiously hidden behind the black beard, which nevertheless was thin, each hair coming thin and fine, singly, from the sallow, slightly translucent skin. In the same way his moustache made a thin black line round his mouth. His eyes were wide open, very black, and of no legible expression. He watched the two women coming down the crowded, dreary room, as if he did not see them. His eyes seemed too wide.

It was a cold day, and Daphne was huddled in a black sealskin coat with a skunk collar pulled up to her ears, and a dull gold cap with wings pulled down on her brow. Lady Beveridge wore her sable coat, and had that odd, untidy elegance which was natural to her, rather like a ruffled chicken.

Daphne was upset by the hospital. She looked from right to left in spite of herself, and everything gave her a dull feeling of horror: the terror of these sick, wounded enemy men. She loomed tall and obtrusive in her furs by the bed, her little mother at her side.

'I hope you don't mind my coming!' she said in German to the sick man. Her tongue felt rusty, speaking the language.

'Who is it then?' he asked.

'It is my daughter, Lady Daphne. You remembered ME, Lady Beveridge! This is my daughter, whom you knew in Saxony. She was so sorry to hear you were wounded.'

The black eyes rested on the little lady. Then they returned to the looming figure of Daphne. And a certain fear grew on the low, sick brow. It was evident the presence loomed and frightened him. He turned his face aside. Daphne noticed how his fine black hair grew uncut over his small, animal ears.

'You don't remember me, Count Dionys?' she said dully.

'Yes,' he said. But he kept his face averted.

She stood there feeling confused and miserable, as if she had made a faux pas in coming.

'Would you rather be left alone?' she said. 'I'm sorry.'

Her voice was monotonous. She felt suddenly stifled in her closed furs, and threw her coat open, showing her thin white throat and plain black slip dress on her flat breast. He turned again unwillingly to look at her. He looked at her as if she were some strange creature standing near him.

'Good-bye,' she said. 'Do get better.'

She was looking at him with a queer, slanting, downward look of

9

her heavy eyes as she turned away. She was still a little red round the eyes, with nervous exhaustion.

'You are so tall,' he said, still frightened.

'I was always tall,' she replied, turning half to him again.

'And I, small,' he said.

'I am so glad you are getting better,' she said.

'I am not glad,' he said.

'Why? I'm sure you are. Just as we are glad because we want you to get better.'

'Thank you,' he said. 'I have wished to die.'

'Don't do that, Count Dionys. Do get better,' she said, in the rather deep, laconic manner of her girlhood. He looked at her with a farther look of recognition. But his short, rather pointed nose was lifted with the disgust and weariness of pain, his brows were tense. He watched her with that curious flame of suffering which is forced to give a little outside attention, but which speaks only to itself.

'Why did they not let me die?' he said. 'I wanted death now.'

'No,' she said. 'You mustn't. You must live. If we CAN live we must.'

'I wanted death,' he said.

'Ah, well,' she said, 'even death we can't have when we want it, or when we think we want it.'

'That is true,' he said, watching her with the same wide black eyes. 'Please to sit down. You are too tall as you stand.'

It was evident he was a little frightened still by her looming, overhanging figure.

'I am sorry I am too tall,' she said, taking a chair which a man-nurse had brought her. Lady Beveridge had gone away to speak with the men. Daphne sat down, not knowing what to say further. The pitch-black look in the Count's wide eyes puzzled her.

'Why do you come here? Why does your lady mother come?' he said.

'To see if we can do anything,' she answered.

'When I am well, I will thank your ladyship.'

'All right,' she replied. 'When you are well I will let my lord the Count thank me. Please do get well.'

'We are enemies,' he said.

'Who? You and I and my mother?'

10

'Are we not? The most difficult thing is to be sure of anything. If they had let me die!'

'That is at least ungrateful, Count Dionys.'

'Lady Daphne! Yes. Lady Daphne! Beautiful, the name is. You are always called Lady Daphne? I remember you were so bright a maiden.'

'More or less,' she said, answering his question.

'Ach! We should all have new names now. I thought of a name for myself, but I have forgotten it. No longer Johann Dionys. That is shot away. I am Karl or Wilhelm or Ernst or Georg. Those are names I hate. Do you hate them?'

'I don't like them — but I don't hate them. And you mustn't leave off being Count Johann Dionys. If you do I shall have to leave off being Daphne. I like your name so much.'

'Lady Daphne! Lady Daphne!' he repeated. 'Yes, it rings well, it sounds beautiful to me. I think I talk foolishly. I hear myself talking foolishly to you.' He looked at her anxiously.

'Not at all,' she said.

'Ach! I have a head on my shoulders that is like a child's windmill, and I can't prevent its making foolish words. Please to go away, not to hear me. I can hear myself.'

'Can't I do anything for you?' she asked.

'No, no! No, no! If I could be buried deep, very deep down, where everything is forgotten! But they draw me up, back to the surface. I would not mind if they buried me alive, if it were very deep, and dark, and the earth heavy above.'

'Don't say that,' she replied, rising.

'No, I am saying it when I don't wish to say it. Why am I here? Why am I here? Why have I survived into this? Why can I not stop talking?'

He turned his face aside. The black, fine, elfish hair was so long, and pushed up in tufts from the smooth brown nape of his neck. Daphne looked at him in sorrow. He could not turn his body. He could only move his head. And he lay with his face hard averted, the fine hair of his beard coming up strange from under his chin and from his throat, up to the socket of his ear. He lay quite still in this position. And she turned away, looking for her mother. She had suddenly realized that the bonds, the connexions between him and his life in the world had broken, and he lay there, a bit of loose, palpitating humanity, shot away from the body of humanity.

It was ten days before she went to the hospital again. She had wanted never to go again, to forget him, as one tries to forget incurable things. But she could not forget him. He came again and again into her mind. She had to go back. She had heard that he was recovering very slowly.

He looked really better. His eyes were not so wide open, they had lost that black, inky exposure which had given him such an unnatural look, unpleasant. He watched her guardedly. She had taken off her furs, and wore only her dress and a dark, soft feather toque.

'How are you?' she said, keeping her face averted, unwilling to meet his eyes.

'Thank you, I am better. The nights are not so long.'

She shuddered, knowing what long nights meant. He saw the worn look in her face too, the reddened rims of her eyes.

'Are you not well? Have you some trouble?' he asked her.

'No, no,' she answered.

She had brought a handful of pinky, daisy-shaped flowers.

'Do you care for flowers?' she asked.

He looked at them. Then he slowly shook his head.

'No,' he said. 'If I am on horseback, riding through the marshes or through the hills, I like to see them below me. But not here. Not now. Please do not bring flowers into this grave. Even in gardens, I do not like them. When they are upholstery to human life.'

'I will take them away again,' she said.

'Please do. Please give them to the nurse.'

Daphne paused.

'Perhaps,' she said, 'you wish I would not come to disturb you.'

He looked into her face.

'No,' he said. 'You are like a flower behind a rock, near an icy water. No, you do not live too much. I am afraid I cannot talk sensibly. I wish to hold my mouth shut. If I open it, I talk this absurdity. It escapes from my mouth.'

'It is not so very absurd,' she said.

But he was silent — looking away from her.

'I want you to tell me if there is really nothing I can do for you,' she said.

'Nothing,' he answered.

12

'If I can write any letter for you.'

'None,' he answered.

'But your wife and your two children. Do they know where you are?'

'I should think not.'

'And where are they?'

'I do not know. Probably they are in Hungary.'

'Not at your home?'

'My castle was burnt down in a riot. My wife went to Hungary with the children. She has her relatives there. She went away from me. I wished it too. Alas for her, I wished to be dead. Pardon me the personal tone.'

Daphne looked down at him — the queer, obstinate little fellow.

'But you have somebody you wish to tell — somebody you want to hear from?'

'Nobody. Nobody. I wish the bullet had gone through my heart. I wish to be dead. It is only I have a devil in my body that will not die.'

She looked at him as he lay with closed, averted face.

'Surely it is not a devil which keeps you alive,' she said. 'It is something good.'

'No, a devil,' he said.

She sat looking at him with a long, slow, wondering look.

'Must one hate a devil that makes one live?' she asked.

He turned his eyes to her with a touch of a satiric smile.

'If one lives, no,' he said.

She looked away from him the moment he looked at her. For her life she could not have met his dark eyes direct.

She left him, and he lay still. He neither read nor talked throughout the long winter nights and the short winter days. He only lay for hours with black, open eyes, seeing everything around with a touch of disgust, and heeding nothing.

Daphne went to see him now and then. She never forgot him for long. He seemed to come into her mind suddenly, as if by sorcery.

One day he said to her:

'I see you are married. May I ask you who is your husband?'

She told him. She had had a letter also from Basil. The Count smiled slowly.

'You can look forward,' he said, 'to a happy reunion and new, lovely children, Lady Daphne. Is it not so?'

'Yes, of course,' she said.

'But you are ill,' he said to her.

'Yes — rather ill.'

'Of what?'

'Oh!' she answered fretfully, turning her face aside. 'They talk about lungs.' She hated speaking of it. 'Why, how do you know I am ill?' she added quickly.

Again he smiled slowly.

'I see it in your face, and hear it in your voice. One would say the Evil One had cast a spell on you.'

'Oh no,' she said hastily. 'But do I look ill?'

'Yes. You look as if something had struck you across the face, and you could not forget it.'

'Nothing has,' she said. 'Unless it's the war.'

'The war!' he repeated.

'Oh, well, don't let us talk of it,' she said.

Another time he said to her:

'The year has turned — the sun must shine at last, even in England. I am afraid of getting well too soon. I am a prisoner, am I not? But I wish the sun would shine. I wish the sun would shine on my face.'

'You won't always be a prisoner. The war will end. And the sun DOES shine even in the winter in England,' she said.

'I wish it would shine on my face,' he said.

So that when in February there came a blue, bright morning, the morning that suggests yellow crocuses and the smell of a mezereon tree and the smell of damp, warm earth, Daphne hastily got a taxi and drove out to the hospital.

'You have come to put me in the sun,' he said the moment he saw her.

'Yes, that's what I came for,' she said.

She spoke to the matron, and had his bed carried out where there was a big window that came low. There he was put full in the sun. Turning, he could see the blue sky and the twinkling tops of purplish, bare trees.

'The world! The world!' he murmured.

14

He lay with his eyes shut, and the sun on his swarthy, transparent, immobile face. The breath came and went through his nostrils invisibly. Daphne wondered how he could lie so still, how he could look so immobile. It was true as her mother had said: he looked as if he had been cast in the mould when the metal was white hot, all his lines were so clean. So small, he was, and in his way perfect.

Suddenly his dark eyes opened and caught her looking.

'The sun makes even anger open like a flower,' he said.

'Whose anger?' she said.

'I don't know. But I can make flowers, looking through my eyelashes. Do you know how?'

'You mean rainbows?'

'Yes, flowers.'

And she saw him, with a curious smile on his lips, looking through his almost closed eyelids at the sun.

'The sun is neither English nor German nor Bohemian,' he said. 'I am a subject of the sun. I belong to the fire-worshippers.'

'Do you?' she replied.

'Yes, truly, by tradition.' He looked at her smiling. 'You stand there like a flower that will melt,' he added.

She smiled slowly at him with a slow, cautious look of her eyes, as if she feared something.

'I am much more solid than you imagine,' she said.

Still he watched her.

'One day,' he said, 'before I go, let me wrap your hair round my hands, will you?' He lifted his thin, short, dark hands. 'Let me wrap your hair round my hands, like a bandage. They hurt me. I don't know what it is. I think it is all the gun explosions. But if you let me wrap your hair round my hands. You know, it is the hermetic gold — but so much of water in it, of the moon. That will soothe my hands. One day, will you?'

'Let us wait till the day comes,' she said.

'Yes,' he answered, and was still again.

'It troubles me,' he said after a while, 'that I complain like a child, and ask for things. I feel I have lost my manhood for the time being. The continual explosions of guns and shells! It seems to have driven my soul out of me like a bird frightened away at last. But it will come back, you know. And I am so grateful to you; you are good to me when I am soulless, and you don't take advantage of me. Your soul is quiet and heroic.'

'Don't,' she said. 'Don't talk!'

The expression of shame and anguish and disgust crossed his face.

'It is because I can't help it,' he said. 'I have lost my soul, and I can't stop talking to you. I can't stop. But I don't talk to anyone else. I try not to talk, but I can't prevent it. Do you draw the words out of me?'

Her wide, green-blue eyes seemed like the heart of some curious, full-open flower, some Christmas rose with its petals of snow and flush. Her hair glinted heavy, like water-gold. She stood there passive and indomitable with the wide-eyed persistence of her wintry, blond nature.

Another day when she came to see him, he watched her for a time, then he said:

'Do they all tell you you are lovely, you are beautiful?'

'Not quite all,' she replied.

'But your husband?'

'He has said so.'

'Is he gentle? Is he tender? Is he a dear lover?'

She turned her face aside, displeased.

'Yes,' she replied curtly.

He did not answer. And when she looked again he was lying with his eyes shut, a faint smile seeming to curl round his short, transparent nose. She could faintly see the flesh through his beard, as water through reeds. His black hair was brushed smooth as glass, his black eyebrows glinted like a curve of black glass on the swarthy opalescence of his brow.

Suddenly he spoke, without opening his eyes.

'You have been very kind to me,' he said.

'Have I? Nothing to speak of.'

He opened his eyes and looked at her.

'Everything finds its mate,' he said. 'The ermine and the pole-cat and the buzzard. One thinks so often that only the dove and the nightingale and the stag with his antlers have gentle mates. But the pole-cat and the ice-bears of the north have their mates. And a white she-bear lies with her cubs under a rock as a snake lies hidden, and the male bear slowly

16

swims back from the sea, like a clot of snow or a shadow of a white cloud passing on the speckled sea. I have seen her too, and I did not shoot her, nor him when he landed with fish in his mouth, wading wet and slow and yellow-white over the black stones.'

'You have been in the North Sea?'

'Yes. And with the Eskimo in Siberia, and across the Tundras. And a white sea-hawk makes a nest on a high stone, and sometimes looks out with her white head over the edge of the rocks. It is not only a world of men, Lady Daphne.'

'Not by any means,' said she.

'Else it were a sorry place.'

'It is bad enough,' said she.

'Foxes have their holes. They have even their mates, Lady Daphne, that they bark to and are answered. And an adder finds his female. Psanek means an outlaw; did you know?'

'I did not.'

'Outlaws, and brigands, have often the finest woman-mates.'

'They do,' she said.

'I will be Psanek, Lady Daphne. I will not be Johann Dionys any more, I will be Psanek. The law has shot me through.'

'You might be Psanek and Johann and Dionys as well,' she said.

'With the sun on my face? Maybe,' he said, looking to the sun.

There were some lovely days in the spring of 1918. In March the Count was able to get up. They dressed him in a simple, dark-blue uniform. He was not very thin, only swarthy-transparent, now his beard was shaven and his hair was cut. His smallness made him noticeable, but he was masculine, perfect in his small stature. All the smiling dapperness that had made him seem like a monkey to Daphne when she was a girl had gone now. His eyes were dark and haughty; he seemed to keep inside his own reserves, speaking to nobody if he could help it, neither to the nurses nor the visitors nor to his fellow-prisoners, fellow-officers. He seemed to put a shadow between himself and them, and from across this shadow he looked with his dark, beautifully-fringed eyes, as a proud little beast from the shadow of its lair. Only to Daphne he laughed and chatted.

She sat with him one day in March on the terrace of the hospital, on a morning when white clouds went endlessly and magnificently about a blue sky, and the sunshine felt warm after the blots of shadow.

'When you had a birthday, and you were seventeen, didn't I give you a thimble?' he asked her.

'Yes. I have it still.'

'With a gold snake at the bottom, and a Mary-beetle of green stone at the top, to push the needle with.'

'Yes.'

'Do you ever use it?'

'No. I sew rarely.'

'Would it displease you to sew something for me?'

'You won't admire my stitches. What would you wish me to sew?'

'Sew me a shirt that I can wear. I have never before worn shirts from a shop, with a maker's name inside. It is very distasteful to me.'

She looked at him — his haughty little brows.

'Shall I ask my maid to do it?' she said.

'Oh, please, no! Oh, please, no, do not trouble. No, please, I would not want it unless you sewed it yourself, with the Psanek thimble.'

She paused before she answered. Then came her slow:

'Why?'

He turned and looked at her with dark, searching eyes.

'I have no reason,' he said, rather haughtily.

She left the matter there. For two weeks she did not go to see him. Then suddenly one day she took the bus down Oxford Street and bought some fine white flannel. She decided he must wear flannel.

That afternoon she drove out to Hurst Place. She found him sitting on the terrace, looking across the garden at the red suburb of London smoking fumily in the near distance, interrupted by patches of uncovered ground and a flat, tin-roofed laundry.

'Will you give me measurements for your shirt?' she said.

'The number of the neck-band of this English shirt is fifteen. If you ask the matron she will give you the measurement. It is a little too large, too long in the sleeves, you see,' and he shook his shirt cuff over his wrist. 'Also too long altogether.'

'Mine will probably be unwearable when I've made them,' said she.

'Oh no. Let your maid direct you. But please do not let her sew them.'

'Will you tell me why you want me to do it?'

'Because I am a prisoner, in other people's clothes, and I have

18

nothing of my own. All the things I touch are distasteful to me. If your maid sews for me, it will still be the same. Only you might give me what I want, something that buttons round my throat and on my wrists.'

'And in Germany — or in Austria?'

'My mother sewed for me. And after her, my mother's sister, who was the head of my house.'

'Not your wife?'

'Naturally not. She would have been insulted. She was never more than a guest in my house. In my family there are old traditions — but with me they have come to an end. I had best try to revive them.'

'Beginning with traditions of shirts?'

'Yes. In our family the shirt should be made and washed by a woman of our own blood: but when we marry, by the wife. So when I married I had sixty shirts, and many other things — sewn by my mother and my aunt, all with my initial, and the ladybird, which is our crest.'

'And where did they put the initial?'

'Here!' He put his finger on the back of his neck, on the swarthy, transparent skin. 'I fancy I can feel the embroidered ladybird still. On our linen we had no crown: only the ladybird.'

She was silent, thinking.

'You will forgive what I ask you?' he said, 'since I am a prisoner and can do no other, and since fate has made you so that you understand the world as I understand it. It is not really indelicate, what I ask you. There will be a ladybird on your finger when you sew, and those who wear the ladybird understand.'

'I suppose,' she mused, 'it is as bad to have your bee in your shirt as in your bonnet.'

He looked at her with round eyes.

'Don't you know what it is to have a bee in your bonnet?' she said.

'No.'

'To have a bee buzzing among your hair! To be out of your wits,' she smiled at him.

'So!' he said. 'Ah, the Psaneks have had a ladybird in their bonnets for many hundred years.'

'Quite, quite mad,' she said.

'It may be,' he answered. 'But with my wife I was quite sane for ten years. Now give me the madness of the ladybird. The world I was sane about has gone raving. The ladybird I was mad with is wise still.'

'At least, when I sew the shirts, if I sew them,' she said, 'I shall have the ladybird at my finger's end.'

'You want to laugh at me.'

'But surely you know you are funny, with your family insect.'

'My family insect? Now you want to be rude to me.'

'How many spots must it have?'

'Seven.'

'Three on each wing. And what do I do with the odd one?'

'You put that one between its teeth, like the cake for Cerebus.'

'I'll remember that.'

When she brought the first shirt, she gave it to the matron. Then she found Count Dionys sitting on the terrace. It was a beautiful spring day. Near at hand were tall elm trees and some rooks cawing.

'What a lovely day!' she said. 'Are you liking the world any better?'

'The world?' he said, looking up at her with the same old discontent and disgust on his fine, transparent nose.

'Yes,' she replied, a shadow coming over her face.

'Is this the world — all those little red-brick boxes in rows, where couples of little people live, who decree my destiny?'

'You don't like England?'

'Ah, England! Little houses like little boxes, each with its domestic Englishman and his domestic wife, each ruling the world because all are alike, so alike.'

'But England isn't all houses.'

'Fields then! Little fields with innumerable hedges. Like a net with an irregular mesh, pinned down over this island and everything under the net. Ah, Lady Daphne, forgive me. I am ungrateful. I am so full of bile, of spleen, you say. My only wisdom is to keep my mouth shut.'

'Why do you hate everything?' she said, her own face going bitter.

'Not everything. If I were free! If I were outside the law. Ah, Lady Daphne, how does one get outside the law?'

'By going inside oneself,' she said. 'Not outside.'

His face took on a greater expression of disgust.

'No, no. I am a man, I am a man, even if I am little. I am not a spirit,

20

that coils itself inside a shell. In my soul is anger, anger, anger. Give me room for my anger. Give me room for that.'

His black eyes looked keenly into hers. She rolled her eyes as if in a half-trance. And in a monotonous, tranced voice she said:

'Much better get over your anger. And WHY are you angry?'

'There is no why. If it were love, you would not ask me, why do you love? But it is anger, anger, anger. What else can I call it? And there is no why.'

Again he looked at her with his dark, sharp, questioning, tormented eyes.

'Can't you get rid of it?' she said, looking aside.

'If a shell exploded and blew me into a thousand fragments,' he said, 'it would not destroy the anger that is in me. I know that. No, it will never dissipate. And to die is no release. The anger goes on gnashing and whimpering in death. Lady Daphne, Lady Daphne, we have used up all the love, and this is what is left.'

'Perhaps YOU have used up all your love,' she replied. 'You are not everybody.'

'I know it. I speak for me and you.'

'Not for me,' she said rapidly.

He did not answer, and they remained silent.

At length she turned her eyes slowly to him.

'Why do you say you speak for me?' she said, in an accusing tone.

'Pardon me. I was hasty.'

But a faint touch of superciliousness in his tone showed he meant what he had said. She mused, her brow cold and stony.

'And why do you tell ME about your anger?' she said. 'Will that make it better?'

'Even the adder finds his mate. And she has as much poison in her mouth as he.'

She gave a little sudden squirt of laughter.

'Awfully poetic thing to say about me,' she said.

He smiled, but with the same corrosive quality.

'Ah,' he said, 'you are not a dove. You are a wild-cat with open eyes, half dreaming on a bough, in a lonely place, as I have seen her. And I ask myself — What are her memories, then?'

'I wish I were a wild-cat,' she said suddenly.

21

He eyed her shrewdly, and did not answer.

'You want more war?' she said to him bitterly.

'More trenches? More Big Berthas, more shells and poison-gas, more machine-drilled science-manoeuvred so-called armies? Never. Never. I would rather work in a factory that makes boots and shoes. And I would rather deliberately starve to death than work in a factory that makes boots and shoes.'

'Then what do you want?'

'I want my anger to have room to grow.'

'How?'

'I do not know. That is why I sit here, day after day. I wait.'

'For your anger to have room to grow?'

'For that.'

'Good-bye, Count Dionys.'

'Good-bye, Lady Daphne.'

She had determined never to go and see him again. She had no sign from him. Since she had begun the second shirt, she went on with it. And then she hurried to finish it, because she was starting a round of visits that would end in the summer sojourn in Scotland. She intended to post the shirt. But after all, she took it herself.

She found Count Dionys had been removed from Hurst Place to Voynich Hall, where other enemy officers were interned. The being thwarted made her more determined. She took the train next day to go to Voynich Hall.

When he came into the ante-room where he was to receive her, she felt at once the old influence of his silence and his subtle power. His face had still that swarthy-transparent look of one who is unhappy, but his bearing was proud and reserved. He kissed her hand politely, leaving her to speak.

'How are you?' she said. 'I didn't know you were here. I am going away for the summer.'

'I wish you a pleasant time,' he said. They were speaking English.

'I brought the other shirt,' she said. 'It is finished at last.'

'That is a greater honour than I dared expect,' he said.

'I'm afraid it may be more honourable than useful. The other didn't fit, did it?'

'Almost,' he said. 'It fitted the spirit, if not the flesh,' he smiled.

22

'I'd rather it had been the reverse, for once,' she said. 'Sorry.'

'I would not have it one stitch different.'

'Can we sit in the garden?'

'I think we may.'

They sat on a bench. Other prisoners were playing croquet not far off. But these two were left comparatively alone.

'Do you like it better here?' she said.

'I have nothing to complain of,' he said.

'And the anger?'

'It is doing well, I thank you,' he smiled.

'You mean getting better?'

'Making strong roots,' he said, laughing.

'Ah, so long as it only makes roots!' she said.

'And your ladyship, how is she?'

'My ladyship is rather better,' she replied.

'Much better, indeed,' he said, looking into her face.

'Do you mean I LOOK much better?' she asked quickly.

'Very much. It is your beauty you think of. Well, your beauty is almost itself again.'

'Thanks.'

'You brood on your beauty as I on my anger. Ah, your ladyship, be wise, and make friends with your anger. That is the way to let your beauty blossom.'

'I was not unfriendly with you, was I?' she said.

'With me?' His face flickered with a laugh. 'Am I your anger? Your vicar in wrath? So then, be friends with the angry me, your ladyship. I ask nothing better.'

'What is the use,' she said, 'being friends with the ANGRY you? I would much rather be friends with the happy you.'

'That little animal is extinct,' he laughed. 'And I am glad of it.'

'But what remains? Only the angry you? Then it is no use my trying to be friends.'

'You remember, dear Lady Daphne, that the adder does not suck his poison all alone, and the pole-cat knows where to find his she-pole-cat. You remember that each one has his own dear mate,' he laughed. 'Dear, deadly mate.'

'And what if I do remember those bits of natural history, Count Dionys?'

23

'The she-adder is dainty, delicate, and carries her poison lightly. The wild-cat has wonderful green eyes that she closes with memory like a screen. The ice-bear hides like a snake with her cubs, and her snarl is the strangest thing in the world.'

'Have you ever heard me snarl?' she asked suddenly.

He only laughed, and looked away.

They were silent. And immediately the strange thrill of secrecy was between them. Something had gone beyond sadness into another, secret, thrilling communion which she would never admit.

'What do you do all day here?' she asked.

'Play chess, play this foolish croquet, play billiards, and read, and wait, and remember.'

'What do you wait for?'

'I don't know.'

'And what do you remember?'

'Ah, that. Shall I tell you what amuses me? Shall I tell you a secret?'

'Please don't, if it's anything that matters.'

'It matters to nobody but me. Will you hear it?'

'If it does not implicate me in any way.'

'It does not. Well, I am a member of a certain old secret society — no, don't look at me, nothing frightening — only a society like the free-masons.'

'And?'

'And — well, as you know, one is initiated into certain so-called secrets and rites. My family has always been initiated. So I am an initiate too. Does it interest you?'

'Why, of course.'

'Well. I was always rather thrilled by these secrets. Or some of them. Some seemed to me far-fetched. The ones that thrilled me even never had any relation to actual life. When you knew me in Dresden and Prague, you would not have thought me a man invested with awful secret knowledge, now would you?'

'Never.'

'No. It was just a little exciting side-show. And I was a grimacing little society man. But now they become true. It becomes true.'

'The secret knowledge?'

'Yes.'

24

'What, for instance?'

'Take actual fire. It will bore you. Do you want to hear?'

'Go on.'

'This is what I was taught. The true fire is invisible. Flame, and the red fire we see burning, has its back to us. It is running away from us. Does that mean anything to you?'

'Yes.'

'Well then, the yellowness of sunshine — light itself — that is only the glancing aside of the real original fire. You know that is true. There would be no light if there was no refraction, no bits of dust and stuff to turn the dark fire into visibility. You know that's a fact. And that being so, even the sun is dark. It is only his jacket of dust that makes him visible. You know that too. And the true sunbeams coming towards us flow darkly, a moving darkness of the genuine fire. The sun is dark, the sunshine flowing to us is dark. And light is only the inside-turning away of the sun's directness that was coming to us. Does that interest you at all?'

'Yes,' she said dubiously.

'Well, we've got the world inside out. The true living world of fire is dark, throbbing, darker than blood. Our luminous world that we go by is only the reverse of this.'

'Yes, I like that,' she said.

'Well! Now listen. The same with love. This white love that we have is the same. It is only the reverse, the whited sepulchre of the true love. True love is dark, a throbbing together in darkness, like the wild-cat in the night, when the green screen opens and her eyes are on the darkness.'

'No, I don't see that,' she said in a slow, clanging voice.

'You, and your beauty — that is only the inside-out of you. The real you is the wild-cat invisible in the night, with red fire perhaps coming out of its wide, dark eyes. Your beauty is your whited sepulchre.'

'You mean cosmetics,' she said. 'I've got none on today — not even powder.'

He laughed.

'Very good,' he said. 'Consider me. I used to think myself small but handsome, and the ladies used to admire me moderately, never very much. A trim little fellow, you know. Well, that was just the inside-out of me. I am a black tom-cat howling in the night, and it is then that fire comes out of me. This me you look at is my whited sepulchre. What do you say?'

She was looking into his eyes. She could see the darkness swaying in the depths. She perceived the invisible, cat-like fire stirring deep inside them, felt it coming towards her. She turned her face aside. Then he laughed, showing his strong white teeth, that seemed a little too large, rather dreadful.

She rose to go.

'Well,' she said. 'I shall have the summer in which to think about the world inside-out. Do write if there is anything to say. Write to Thoresway. Good-bye!'

'Ah, your eyes!' he said. 'They are like jewels of stone.'

Being away from the Count, she put him out of her mind. Only she was sorry for him a prisoner in that sickening Voynich Hall. But she did not write. Nor did he.

As a matter of fact, her mind was now much more occupied with her husband. All arrangements were being made to effect his exchange. From month to month she looked for his return. And so she thought of him.

Whatever happened to her, she thought about it, thought and thought a great deal. The consciousness of her mind was like tablets of stone weighing her down. And whoever would make a new entry into her must break these tablets of stone piece by piece. So it was that in her own way she thought often enough of the Count's world inside-out. A curious latency stirred in her consciousness that was not yet an idea.

He said her eyes were like jewels of stone. What a horrid thing to say! What did he want her eyes to be like? He wanted them to dilate and become all black pupil, like a cat's at night. She shrank convulsively from the thought, and tightened her breast.

He said her beauty was her whited sepulchre. Even that, she knew what he meant. The invisibility of her he wanted to love. But ah, her pearl-like beauty was so dear to her, and it was so famous in the world.

He said her white love was like moonshine, harmful, the reverse of love. He meant Basil, of course. Basil always said she was the moon. But then Basil loved her for that. The ecstasy of it! She shivered, thinking of her husband. But it had also made her nerve-worn, her husband's love. Ah, nerve-worn.

What then would the Count's love be like? Something so secret and different. She would not be lovely and a queen to him. He hated her loveliness. The wild-cat has its mate. The little wild-cat that he was. Ah!

She caught her breath, determined not to think. When she thought of Count Dionys she felt the world slipping away from her. She would sit in front of a mirror, looking at her wonderful cared-for face that had appeared in so many society magazines. She loved it so, it made her feel so vain. And she looked at her blue-green eyes — the eyes of the wild-cat on a bough. Yes, the lovely blue-green iris drawn tight like a screen. Supposing it should relax. Supposing it should unfold, and open out the dark depths, the dark, dilated pupil! Supposing it should?

Never! She always caught herself back. She felt she might be killed before she could give way to that relaxation that the Count wanted of her. She could not. She just could not. At the very thought of it some hypersensitive nerve started with a great twinge in her breast; she drew back, forced to keep her guard. Ah no, Monsieur le Comte, you shall never take her ladyship off her guard.

She disliked the thought of the Count. An impudent little fellow. An impertinent little fellow! A little madman, really. A little outsider. No, no. She would think of her husband: an adorable, tall, well-bred Englishman, so easy and simple, and with the amused look in his blue eyes. She thought of the cultured, casual trail of his voice. It set her nerves on fire. She thought of his strong, easy body — beautiful, white-fleshed, with the fine springing of warm-brown hair like tiny flames. He was the Dionysos, full of sap, milk and honey, and northern golden wine: he, her husband. Not that little unreal Count. Ah, she dreamed of her husband, of the love-days, and the honeymoon, the lovely, simple intimacy. Ah, the marvellous revelation of that intimacy, when he left himself to her so generously. Ah, she was his wife for this reason, that he had given himself to her so greatly, so generously. Like an ear of corn he was there for her gathering — her husband, her own, lovely, English husband. Ah, when would he come again, when would he come again!

She had letters from him — and how he loved her. Far away, his life was all hers. All hers, flowing to her as the beam flows from a white star right down to us, to our heart. Her lover, her husband.

27

He was now expecting to come home soon. It had all been arranged. 'I hope you won't be disappointed in me when I do get back,' he wrote. 'I am afraid I am no longer the plump and well-looking young man I was. I've got a big scar at the side of my mouth, and I'm as thin as a starved rabbit, and my hair's going grey. Doesn't sound attractive, does it? And it isn't attractive. But once I can get out of this infernal place, and once I can be with you again, I shall come in for my second blooming. The very thought of being quietly in the same house with you, quiet and in peace, makes me realize that if I've been through hell, I have known heaven on earth and can hope to know it again. I am a miserable brute to look at now. But I have faith in you. You will forgive my appearance, and that alone will make me feel handsome.'

She read this letter many times. She was not afraid of his scar or his looks. She would love him all the more.

Since she had started making shirts — those two for the Count had been an enormous labour, even though her maid had come to her assistance forty times: but since she had started making shirts, she thought she might continue. She had some good suitable silk: her husband liked silk underwear.

But she still used the Count's thimble. It was gold outside and silver inside, and was too heavy. A snake was coiled round the base, and at the top, for pressing the needle, was inlet a semi-translucent apple-green stone, perhaps jade, carved like a scarab, with little dots. It was too heavy. But then she sewed so slowly. And she liked to feel her hand heavy, weighted. And as she sewed she thought about her husband, and she felt herself in love with him. She thought of him, how beautiful he was, and how she would love him now he was thin: she would love him all the more. She would love to trace his bones, as if to trace his living skeleton. The thought made her rest her hands in her lap and drift into a muse. Then she felt the weight of the thimble on her finger, and took it off, and sat looking at the green stone. The ladybird. The ladybird. And if only her husband would come soon, soon. It was wanting him that made her so ill. Nothing but that. She had wanted him so badly. She wanted now. Ah, if she could go to him now, and find him, wherever he was, and see him and touch him and take all his love.

As she mused, she put the thimble down in front of her, took up a little silver pencil from her work-basket, and on a bit of blue paper that had been the band of a small skein of silk she wrote the lines of the silly little song

'Wenn ich ein Voglein war'
Und auch zwei Fluglein hatt'
Flag' ich zu dir — '

That was all she could get on her bit of pale-blue paper.

'If I were a little bird
And had two little wings
I'd fly to thee —

Silly enough, in all conscience. But she did not translate it, so it did not seem quite so silly.

At that moment her maid announced Lady Bingham — her husband's sister. Daphne crumpled up the bit of paper in a flurry, and in another minute Primrose, his sister, came in. The newcomer was not a bit like a primrose, being long-faced and clever, smart, but not a bit elegant, in her new clothes.

'Daphne dear, what a domestic scene! I suppose it's rehearsal. Well, you may as well rehearse, he's with Admiral Burns on the Ariadne. Father just heard from the Admiralty: quite fit. He'll be here in a day or two. Splendid, isn't it? And the war is going to end. At least it seems like it. You'll be safe of your man now, dear. Thank heaven when it's all over. What are you sewing?'

'A shirt,' said Daphne.

'A shirt! Why, how clever of you. I should never know which end to begin. Who showed you?'

'Millicent.'

'And how did SHE know? She's no business to know how to sew shirts: nor cushions nor sheets either. Do let me look. Why, how perfectly marvellous you are! — every bit by hand too. Basil isn't worth it, dear, really he isn't. Let him order his shirts in Oxford Street. Your business is to be beautiful, not to sew shirts. What a dear little pin-poppet, or rather needle-woman! I say, a satire on us, that is. But what a darling, with mother-of-pearl wings to her skirts! And darling little gold-eyed needles inside her. You screw her head off, and you find she's full of pins and needles. Woman for you! Mother says won't you come to lunch tomorrow. And won't you come to Brassey's to tea with me at this minute. Do, there's a dear. I've got a taxi.'

29

Daphne bundled her sewing loosely together.

When she tried to do a bit more, two days later, she could not find her thimble. She asked her maid, whom she could absolutely trust. The girl had not seen it. She searched everywhere. She asked her nurse — who was now her housekeeper — and footman. No, nobody had seen it. Daphne even asked her sister-in-law.

'Thimble, darling? No, I don't remember a thimble. I remember a dear little needle-lady, whom I thought such a precious satire on us women. I didn't notice a thimble.'

Poor Daphne wandered about in a muse. She did not want to believe it lost. It had been like a talisman to her. She tried to forget it. Her husband was coming, quite soon, quite soon. But she could not raise herself to joy. She had lost her thimble. It was as if Count Dionys accused her in her sleep of something, she did not quite know what.

And though she did not really want to go to Voynich Hall, yet like a fatality she went, like one doomed. It was already late autumn, and some lovely days. This was the last of the lovely days. She was told that Count Dionys was in the small park, finding chestnuts. She went to look for him. Yes, there he was in his blue uniform stooping over the brilliant yellow leaves of the sweet chestnut tree, that lay around him like a fallen nimbus of glowing yellow, under his feet, as he kicked and rustled, looking for the chestnut burrs. And with his short, brown hands he was pulling out the small chestnuts and putting them in his pockets. But as she approached he peeled a nut to eat it. His teeth were white and powerful.

'You remind me of a squirrel laying in a winter store,' said she.

'Ah, Lady Daphne — I was thinking and did not hear you.'

'I thought you were gathering chestnuts — even eating them.'

'Also!' he laughed. He had a dark, sudden charm when he laughed, showing his rather large white teeth. She was not quite sure whether she found him a little repulsive.

'Were you REALLY thinking?' she said, in her slow, resonant way.

'Very truly.'

'And weren't you enjoying the chestnut a bit?'

'Very much. Like sweet milk. Excellent, excellent.' He had the fragments of the nut between his teeth, and bit them finely. 'Will you take one too.' He held out the little, pointed brown nuts on the palm of his hand.

She looked at them doubtfully.

'Are they as tough as they always were?' she said.

'No, they are fresh and good. Wait, I will peel one for you.'

They strayed about through the thin clump of trees.

'You have had a pleasant summer; you are strong?'

'Almost QUITE strong,' said she. 'Lovely summer, thanks. I suppose it's no good asking you if you have been happy?'

'Happy?' He looked at her direct. His eyes were black, and seemed to examine her. She always felt he had a little contempt of her. 'Oh yes,' he said, smiling. 'I have been very happy.'

'So glad.'

They drifted a little farther, and he picked up an apple-green chestnut burr out of the yellow-brown leaves, handling it with sensitive fingers that still suggested paws to her.

'How did you succeed in being happy?' she said.

'How shall I tell you? I felt that the same power which put up the mountains could pull them down again — no matter how long it took.'

'And was that all?'

'Was it not enough?'

'I should say decidedly too little.'

He laughed broadly, showing the strong, negroid teeth.

'You do not know all it means,' he said.

'The thought that the mountains were going to be pulled down?' she said. 'It will be so long after my day.'

'Ah, you are bored,' he said. 'But I— I found the God who pulls things down: especially the things that men have put up. Do they not say that life is a search after God, Lady Daphne? I have found my God.'

'The god of destruction,' she said, blanching.

'Yes — not the devil of destruction, but the god of destruction. The blessed god of destruction. It is strange' — he stood before her, looking up at her — 'but I have found my God. The god of anger, who throws down the steeples and the factory chimneys. Ah, Lady Daphne, he is a man's God, he is a man's God. I have found my God, Lady Daphne.'

'Apparently. And how are you going to serve him?'

A naive glow transfigured his face.

'Oh, I will help. With my heart I will help while I can do nothing with my hands. I say to my heart: Beat, hammer, beat with little strokes. Beat, hammer of God, beat them down. Beat it all down.'

31

Her brows knitted, her face took on a look of discontent.

'Beat what down?' she asked harshly.

'The world, the world of man. Not the trees — these chestnuts, for example' — he looked up at them, at the tufts and loose pinions of yellow — 'not these — nor the chattering sorcerers, the squirrels — nor the hawk that comes. Not those.'

'You mean beat England?' she said.

'Ah, no. Ah, no. Not England any more than Germany — perhaps not as much. Not Europe any more than Asia.'

'Just the end of the world?'

'No, no. No, no. What grudge have I against a world where little chestnuts are so sweet as these! Do you like yours? Will you take another?'

'No, thanks.'

'What grudge have I against a world where even the hedges are full of berries, bunches of black berries that hang down, and red berries that thrust up. Never would I hate the world. But the world of man. Lady Daphne' — his voice sank to a whisper — 'I HATE IT. Zzz!' he hissed. 'Strike, little heart! Strike, strike, hit, smite! Oh, Lady Daphne!' — his eyes dilated with a ring of fire.

'What?' she said, scared.

'I believe in the power of my red, dark heart. God has put the hammer in my breast — the little eternal hammer. Hit — hit — hit! It hits on the world of man. It hits, it hits! And it hears the thin sound of cracking. The thin sound of cracking. Hark!'

He stood still and made her listen. It was late afternoon. The strange laugh of his face made the air seem dark to her. And she could easily have believed that she heard a faint, fine shivering, cracking, through the air, a delicate crackling noise.

'You hear it? Yes? Oh, may I live long! May I live long, so that my hammer may strike and strike, and the cracks go deeper, deeper! Ah, the world of man! Ah, the joy, the passion in every heart-beat! Strike home, strike true, strike sure. Strike to destroy it. Strike! Strike! To destroy the world of man. Ah, God. Ah, God, prisoner of peace. Do I not know you, Lady Daphne? Do I not? Do I not?'

She was silent for some moments, looking away at the twinkling lights of a station beyond.

32

'Not the white plucked lily of your body. I have gathered no flower for my ostentatious life. But in the cold dark, your lily root, Lady Daphne. Ah, yes, you will know it all your life, that I know where your root lies buried, with its sad, sad quick of life. What does it matter!'

They had walked slowly towards the house. She was silent. Then at last she said, in a peculiar voice:

'And you would never want to kiss me?'

'Ah, no!' he answered sharply.

She held out her hand.

'Good-bye, Count Dionys,' she drawled, fashionably. He bowed over her hand, but did not kiss it.

'Good-bye, Lady Daphne.'

She went away, with her brow set hard. And henceforth she thought only of her husband, of Basil. She made the Count die out of her. Basil was coming, he was near. He was coming back from the East, from war and death. Ah, he had been through awful fire of experience. He would be something new, something she did not know. He was something new, a stronger lover who had been through terrible fire, and had come out strange and new, like a god. Ah, new and terrible his love would be, pure and intensified by the awful fire of suffering. A new lover — a new bridegroom — a new, supernatural wedding-night. She shivered in anticipation, waiting for her husband. She hardly noticed the wild excitement of the Armistice. She was waiting for something more wonderful to her.

And yet the moment she heard his voice on the telephone, her heart contracted with fear. It was his well-known voice, deliberate, diffident, almost drawling, with the same subtle suggestion of deference, and the rather exaggerated Cambridge intonation, up and down. But there was a difference, a new icy note that went through her veins like death.

'Is that you, Daphne? I shall be with you in half an hour. Is that all right for you? Yes, I've just landed, and shall come straight to you. Yes, a taxi. Shall I be too sudden for you, darling? No? Good, oh good! Half an hour, then! I say, Daphne? There won't be anyone else there, will there? Quite alone! Good! I can ring up Dad afterwards. Yes, splendid, splendid. Sure you're all right, my darling? I'm at death's door till I see you. Yes. Good-bye — half an hour. Good-bye.'

When Daphne had hung up the receiver she sat down almost in a faint. What was it that so frightened her? His terrible, terrible altered voice, like cold, blue steel. She had no time to think. She rang for her maid.

'Oh, my lady, it isn't bad news?' cried Millicent, when she caught sight of her mistress white as death.

'No, good news. Major Apsley will be here in half an hour. Help me to dress. Ring to Murry's first to send in some roses, red ones, and some lilac-coloured iris — two dozen of each, at once.'

Daphne went to her room. She didn't know what to wear, she didn't know how she wanted her hair dressed. She spoke hastily to her maid. She chose a violet-coloured dress. She did not know what she was doing. In the middle of dressing the flowers came, and she left off to put them in the bowls. So that when she heard his voice in the hall, she was still standing in front of the mirror reddening her lips and wiping it away again.

'Major Apsley, my lady!' murmured the maid, in excitement.

'Yes, I can hear. Go and tell him I shall be one minute.'

Daphne's voice had become slow and sonorous, like bronze, as it always did when she was upset. Her face looked almost haggard, and in vain she dabbed with the rouge.

'How does he look?' she asked curtly, when her maid came back.

'A long scar here,' said the maid, and she drew her finger from the left-hand corner of her mouth into her cheek, slanting downwards.

'Make him look very different?' asked Daphne.

'Not so VERY different, my lady,' said Millicent gently. 'His eyes are the same, I think.' The girl also was distressed.

'All right,' said Daphne. She looked at herself a long, last look as she turned away from the mirror. The sight of her own face made her feel almost sick. She had seen so much of herself. And yet even now she was fascinated by the heavy droop of her lilac-veined lids over her slow, strange, large, green-blue eyes. They WERE mysterious-looking. And she gave herself a long, sideways glance, curious and Chinese. How was it possible there was a touch of the Chinese in her face? — she so purely an English blonde, an Aphrodite of the foam, as Basil had called her in poetry. Ah well! She left off her thoughts and went through the hall to the drawing-room.

He was standing nervously in the middle of the room in his uniform. She hardly glanced at his face — and saw only the scar.

34

'Hullo, Daphne,' he said, in a voice full of the expected emotion. He stepped forward and took her in his arms, and kissed her forehead.

'So glad! So glad it's happened at last,' she said, hiding her tears.

'So glad what has happened, darling?' he asked, in his deliberate manner.

'That you're back.' Her voice had the bronze resonance, she spoke rather fast.

'Yes, I'm back, Daphne darling — as much of me as there is to bring back.'

'Why?' she said. 'You've come back whole, surely?' She was frightened.

'Yes, apparently I have. Apparently. But don't let's talk of that. Let's talk of you, darling. How are you? Let me look at you. You are thinner, you are older. But you are more wonderful than ever. Far more wonderful.'

'How?' said she.

'I can't exactly say how. You were only a girl. Now you are a woman. I suppose it's all that's happened. But you are wonderful as a woman, Daphne darling — more wonderful than all that's happened. I couldn't have believed you'd be so wonderful. I'd forgotten — or else I'd never known. I say, I'm a lucky chap really. Here I am, alive and well, and I've got you for a wife. It's brought you out like a flower. I say, darling, there is more now than Venus of the foam — grander. How beautiful you are! But you look like the beauty of all life — as if you were moon-mother of the world — Aphrodite. God is good to me after all, darling. I ought never to utter a single complaint. How lovely you are — how lovely you are, my darling! I'd forgotten you — and I thought I knew you so well. Is it true that you belong to me? Are you really mine?'

They were seated on the yellow sofa. He was holding her hand, and his eyes were going up and down, from her face to her throat and her breast. The sound of his words, and the strong, cold desire in his voice excited her, pleased her, and made her heart freeze. She turned and looked into his light blue eyes. They had no longer the amused light, nor the young look. They burned with a hard, focused light, whitish.

'It's all right. You are mine, aren't you, Daphne darling?' came his cultured, musical voice, that had always the well-bred twang of diffidence.

35

She looked back into his eyes.

'Yes, I am yours,' she said, from the lips.

'Darling! Darling!' he murmured, kissing her hand.

Her heart beat suddenly so terribly, as if her breast would be ruptured, and she rose in one movement and went across the room. She leaned her hand on the mantelpiece and looked down at the electric fire. She could hear the faint, faint noise of it. There was silence for a few moments.

Then she turned and looked at him. He was watching her intently. His face was gaunt, and there was a curious deathly sub-pallor, though his cheeks were not white. The scar ran livid from the side of his mouth. It was not so very big. But it seemed like a scar in him himself, in his brain, as it were. In his eyes was that hard, white, focused light that fascinated her and was terrible to her. He was different. He was like death; like risen death. She felt she dared not touch him. White death was still upon him. She could tell that he shrank with a kind of agony from contact. 'Touch me not, I am not yet ascended unto the Father.' Yet for contact he had come. Something, someone seemed to be looking over his shoulder. His own young ghost looking over his shoulder. Oh, God! She closed her eyes, seeming to swoon. He remained leaning forward on the sofa, watching her.

'Aren't you well, darling?' he asked. There was a strange, incomprehensible coldness in his very fire. He did not move to come near her.

'Yes, I'm well. It is only that after all it is so sudden. Let me get used to you,' she said, turning aside her face from him. She felt utterly like a victim of his white, awful face.

'I suppose I must be a bit of a shock to you,' he said. 'I hope you won't leave off loving me. It won't be that, will it?'

The strange coldness in his voice! And yet the white, uncanny fire.

'No, I shan't leave off loving you,' she admitted, in a low tone, as if almost ashamed. She DARED not have said otherwise. And the saying it made it true.

'Ah, if you're sure of that,' he said. 'I'm a pretty unlovely sight to behold, I know, with this wound-scar. But if you can forgive it me, darling. Do you think you can?' There was something like compulsion in his tone.

She looked at him, and shivered slightly.

'I love you — more than before,' she said hurriedly.

'Even the scar?' came his terrible voice, inquiring.

She glanced again, with that slow, Chinese side-look, and felt she would die.

'Yes,' she said, looking away at nothingness. It was an awful moment to her. A little, slightly imbecile smile widened on his face.

He suddenly knelt at her feet, and kissed the toe of her slipper, and kissed the instep, and kissed the ankle in the thin black stocking.

'I knew,' he said in a muffled voice. 'I knew you would make good. I knew if I had to kneel, it was before you. I knew you were divine, you were the one — Cybele — Isis. I knew I was your slave. I knew. It has all been just a long initiation. I had to learn how to worship you.'

He kissed her feet again and again, without the slightest self-consciousness, or the slightest misgiving. Then he went back to the sofa, and sat there looking at her, saying:

'It isn't love, it is worship. Love between me and you will be a sacrament, Daphne. That's what I had to learn. You are beyond me. A mystery to me. My God, how great it all is. How marvellous!'

She stood with her hand on the mantelpiece, looking down and not answering. She was frightened — almost horrified: but she was thrilled deep down to her soul. She really felt she could glow white and fill the universe like the moon, like Astarte, like Isis, like Venus. The grandeur of her own pale power. The man religiously worshipped her, not merely amorously. She was ready for him — for the sacrament of his supreme worship.

He sat on the sofa with his hands spread on the yellow brocade and pushing downwards behind him, down between the deep upholstery of the back and the seat. He had long, white hands with pale freckles. And his fingers touched something. With his long white fingers he groped and brought it out. It was the lost thimble. And inside it was the bit of screwed-up blue paper.

'I say, is that YOUR thimble?' he asked.

She started, and went hurriedly forward for it.

'Where was it?' she said, agitated.

But he did not give it to her. He turned it round and pulled out the bit of blue paper. He saw the faint pencil marks on the screwed-up ball, and unrolled the band of paper, and slowly deciphered the verse.

'Wenn ich ein Voglein war'

Und auch zwei Fluglein hatt'

Flog' ich zu dir — '

'How awfully touching that is,' he said. 'A Voglein with two little Fluglein! But what a precious darling child you are! Whom did you want to fly to, if you were a Voglein?' He looked up at her with a curious smile.

'I can't remember,' she said, turning aside her head.

'I hope it was to me,' he said. 'Anyhow, I shall consider it was, and shall love you all the more for it. What a darling child! A Voglein if you please, with two little wings! Why, how beautifully absurd of you, darling!'

He folded the scrap of paper carefully, and put it in his pocket-book, keeping the thimble all the time between his knees.

'Tell me when you lost it, Daphne,' he said, examining the bauble.

'About a month ago — or two months.'

'About a month ago — or two months. And what were you sewing? Do you mind if I ask? I like to think of you then. I was still in that beastly El Hasrun. What were you sewing, darling, two months ago, when you lost your thimble?'

'A shirt.'

'I say, a shirt! Whose shirt?'

'Yours.'

'There. Now we've run it to earth. Were you really sewing a shirt for me! Is it finished? Can I put it on at this minute?'

'That one isn't finished, but the first one is.'

'I say, darling, let me go and put it on. To think I should have it next my skin! I shall feel you all round me, all over me. I say how marvellous that will be! Won't you come?'

'Won't you give me the thimble?' she said.

'Yes, of course. What a noble thimble too! Who gave it you?'

'Count Dionys Psanek.'

'Who was he?'

'A Bohemian Count, in Dresden. He once stayed with us in Thoresway — with a tall wife. Didn't you meet them?'

'I don't think I did. I don't think I did. I don't remember. What was he like?'

'A little man with black hair and a rather low, dark forehead — rather dressy.'

'No, I don't remember him at all. So he gave it you. Well, I wonder where he is now? Probably rotted, poor devil.'

'No, he's interned in Voynich Hall. Mother and I have been to see him several times. He was awfully badly wounded.'

'Poor little beggar! In Voynich Hall! I'll look at him before he goes. Odd thing, to give you a thimble. Odd gift! You were a girl then, though. Do you think he had it made, or do you think he found it in a shop?'

'I think it belonged to the family. The ladybird at the top is part of their crest — and the snake as well, I think.'

'A ladybird! Funny thing for a crest. Americans would call it a bug. I must look at him before he goes. And you were sewing a shirt for me! And then you posted me this little letter into the sofa. Well, I'm awfully glad I received it, and that it didn't go astray in the post, like so many things. "Wenn ich ein Voglein war" — you perfect child! But that is the beauty of a woman like you: you are so superb and beyond worship, and then such an exquisite naive child. Who could help worshipping you and loving you: immortal and mortal together. What, you want the thimble? Here! Wonderful, wonderful, white fingers. Ah, darling, you are more goddess than child, you long, limber Isis with sacred hands. White, white, and immortal! Don't tell me your hands could die, darling: your wonderful Proserpine fingers. They are immortal as February and snowdrops. If you lift your hands the spring comes. I CAN'T help kneeling before you, darling. I am no more than a sacrifice to you, an offering. I WISH I could die in giving myself to you, give you all my blood on your altar, for ever.'

She looked at him with a long, slow look, as he turned his face to her. His face was white with ecstasy. And she was not afraid. Somewhere, saturnine, she knew it was absurd. But she chose not to know. A certain swoon-sleep was on her. With her slow, green-blue eyes she looked down on his ecstasized face, almost benign. But in her right hand unconsciously she held the thimble fast, she only gave him her left hand. He took her hand and rose to his feet in that curious priestly ecstasy which made him more than a man or a soldier, far, far more than a lover to her.

39

Nevertheless, his home-coming made her begin to be ill again. Afterwards, after his love, she had to bear herself in torment. To her shame and her heaviness, she knew she was not strong enough, or pure enough, to bear this awful outpouring adoration-lust. It was not her fault she felt weak and fretful afterwards, as if she wanted to cry and be fretful and petulant, wanted someone to save her. She could not turn to Basil, her husband. After his ecstasy of adoration-lust for her, she recoiled from him. Alas, she was not the goddess, the superb person he named her. She was flawed with the fatal humility of her age. She could not harden her heart and burn her soul pure of this humility, this misgiving. She could not finally believe in her own woman-godhead — only in her own female mortality.

That fierce power of being alone, even with your lover, the fierce power of the woman in excelsis — alas, she could not keep it. She could rise to the height for the time, the incandescent, transcendent, moon-fierce womanhood. But alas, she could not stay intensified and resplendent in her white, womanly powers, her female mystery. She relaxed, she lost her glory, and became fretful. Fretful and ill and never to be soothed. And then naturally her man became ashy and somewhat acrid, while she ached with nerves, and could not eat.

Of course she began to dream about Count Dionys: to yearn wistfully for him. And it was absolutely a fatal thought to her that he was going away. When she thought that — that he was leaving England soon — going away into the dark for ever — then the last spark seemed to die in her. She felt her soul perish, whilst she herself was worn and soulless like a prostitute. A prostitute goddess. And her husband, the gaunt, white, intensified priest of her, who never ceased from being before her like a lust.

'Tomorrow,' she said to him, gathering her last courage and looking at him with a side look, 'I want to go to Voynich Hall.'

'What, to see Count Psanek? Oh, good! Yes, very good! I'll come along as well. I should like very much to see him. I suppose he'll be getting sent back before long.'

It was a fortnight before Christmas, very dark weather. Her husband was in khaki. She wore her black furs and a black lace veil over her face, so that she seemed mysterious. But she lifted the veil and looped it behind, so that it made a frame for her face. She looked very lovely like that — her face pure like the most white hellebore flower, touched with winter pink, amid the blackness of her drapery and furs. Only she was rather too much like the picture of a modern beauty: too much the actual thing. She had half an idea that Dionys would hate her for her effective loveliness. He would see it and hate it. The thought was like a bitter balm to her. For herself, she loved her loveliness almost with obsession.

The Count came cautiously forward, glancing from the lovely figure of Lady Daphne to the gaunt well-bred Major at her side. Daphne was so beautiful in her dark furs, the black lace of her veil thrown back over her close-fitting, dull-gold-threaded hat, and her face fair like a winter flower in a cranny of darkness. But on her face, that was smiling with a slow self-satisfaction of beauty and of knowledge that she was dangling the two men, and setting all the imprisoned officers wildly on the alert, the Count could read that acridity of dissatisfaction and of inefficiency. And he looked away to the livid scar on the Major's cheek.

'Count Dionys, I wanted to bring my husband to see you. May I introduce him to you? Major Apsley — Count Dionys Psanek.'

The two men shook hands rather stiffly.

'I can sympathize with you being fastened up in this place,' said Basil in his slow, easy fashion. 'I hated it, I assure you, out there in the East.'

'But your conditions were much worse than mine,' smiled the Count.

'Well, perhaps they were. But prison is prison, even if it were heaven itself.'

'Lady Apsley has been the one angel of my heaven,' smiled the Count.

'I'm afraid I was as inefficient as most angels,' said she.

The small smile never left the Count's dark face. It was true as she said, he was low-browed, the black hair growing low on his brow, and his eyebrows making a thick bow above his dark eyes, which had again long black lashes. So that the upper part of his face seemed very dusky-black. His nose was small and somewhat translucent. There was a touch of mockery about him, which was intensified even by his small, energetic stature. He was still carefully dressed in the dark-blue uniform, whose shabbiness could not hinder the dark flame of life which seemed to glow through the cloth from his body. He was not

41

thin — but still had a curious swarthy translucency of skin in his low-browed face.

'What would you have been more?' he laughed, making equivocal dark eyes at her.

'Oh, of course, a delivering angel — a cinema heroine,' she replied, closing her eyes and turning her face aside.

All the while the white-faced, tall Major watched the little man with a fixed, half-smiling scrutiny. The Count seemed to notice. He turned to the Englishman.

'I am glad that I can congratulate you, Major Apsley, on your safe and happy return to your home.'

'Thanks. I hope I may be able to congratulate you in the same way before long.'

'Oh yes,' said the Count. 'Before long I shall be shipped back.'

'Have you any news of your family?' interrupted Daphne.

'No news,' he replied briefly, with sudden gravity.

'It seems you'll find a fairish mess out in Austria,' said Basil.

'Yes, probably. It is what we had to expect,' replied the Count.

'Well, I don't know. Sometimes things do turn out for the best. I feel that's as good as true in my case,' said the Major.

'Things have turned out for the best?' said the Count, with an intonation of polite inquiry.

'Yes. Just for me personally, I mean — to put it quite selfishly. After all, what we've learned is that a man can only speak for himself. And I feel it's been dreadful, but it's not been lost. It was like an ordeal one had to go through,' said Basil.

'You mean the war?'

'The war and everything that went with it.'

'And when you've been through the ordeal?' politely inquired the Count.

'Why, you arrive at a higher state of consciousness, and therefore of life. And so, of course, at a higher plane of love. A surprisingly higher plane of love, that you had never suspected the existence of before.'

The Count looked from Basil to Daphne, who was posing her head a little self-consciously.

'Then indeed the war has been a valuable thing,' he said.

'Exactly!' cried Basil. 'I am another man.'

'And Lady Apsley?' queried the Count.

'Oh' — her husband faced round to her — 'she is ABSOLUTELY another woman — and MUCH more wonderful, more marvellous.'

The Count smiled and bowed slightly.

'When we knew her ten years ago, we should have said then that it was impossible,' said he, 'for her to be more wonderful.'

'Oh, quite!' returned the husband. 'It always seems impossible. And the impossible is always happening. As a matter of fact, I think the war has opened another circle of life to us — a wider ring.'

'It may be so,' said the Count.

'You don't feel it so yourself?' The Major looked with his keen, white attention into the dark, low-browed face of the other man. The Count looked smiling at Daphne.

'I am only a prisoner still, Major, therefore I feel my ring quite small.'

'Yes, of course you do. Of course. Well, I do hope you won't be a prisoner much longer. You must be dying to get back into your own country.'

'Yes, I shall be glad to be free. Also,' he smiled. 'I shall miss my prison and my visits from the angels.'

Even Daphne could not be sure he was mocking her. It was evident the visit was unpleasant to him. She could see he did not like Basil. Nay, more, she could feel that the presence of her tall, gaunt, idealistic husband was hateful to the little swarthy man. But he passed it all off in smiles and polite speeches.

On the other hand, Basil was as if fascinated by the Count. He watched him absorbedly all the time, quite forgetting Daphne. She knew this. She knew that she was quite gone out of her husband's consciousness, like a lamp that has been carried away into another room. There he stood completely in the dark, as far as she was concerned, and all his attention focused on the other man. On his pale, gaunt face was a fixed smile of amused attention.

'But don't you get awfully bored,' he said, 'between the visits?'

The Count looked up with an affection of frankness.

'No, I do not,' he said. 'I can brood, you see, on the things that come to pass.'

'I think that's where the harm comes in,' replied the Major. 'One sits and broods, and is cut off from everything, and one loses one's contact with reality. That's the effect it had on me, being a prisoner.'

'Contact with reality — what is that?'

'Well — contact with anybody, really — or anything.'

'Why must one have contact?'

'Well, because one must,' said Basil.

The Count smiled slowly.

'But I can sit and watch fate flowing, like black water, deep down in my own soul,' he said. 'I feel that there, in the dark of my own soul, things are happening.'

'That may be. But whatever happens, it is only one thing, really. It is a contact between your own soul and the soul of one other being, or of many other beings. Nothing else can happen to man. That's how I figured it out for myself. I may be wrong. But that's how I figured it out when I was wounded and a prisoner.'

The Count's face had gone dark and serious.

'But is this contact an aim in itself?' he asked.

'Well' — said the Major — he had taken his degree in philosophy — 'it seems to me it is. It results inevitably in some form of activity. But the cause and the origin and the life-impetus of all action, activity, whether constructive or destructive, seems to me to be in the dynamic contact between human beings. You bring to pass a certain dynamic contact between men, and you get war. Another sort of dynamic contact, and you get them all building a cathedral, as they did in the Middle Ages.'

'But was not the war, or the cathedral, the real aim, and the emotional contact just the means?' said the Count.

'I don't think so,' said the Major, his curious white passion beginning to glow through his face. The three were seated in a little card-room, left alone by courtesy by the other men. Daphne was still draped in her dark, too-becoming drapery. But alas, she sat now ignored by both men. She might just as well have been an ugly little nobody, for all the notice that was taken of her. She sat in the window-seat of the dreary small room with a look of discontent on her exotic, rare face, that was like a delicate white and pink hot-house flower. From time to time she glanced with long, slow looks from man to man: from her husband, whose pallid, intense, white glowing face was pressed forward across

44

the table to the Count, who sat back in his chair, as if in opposition, and whose dark face seemed clubbed together in a dark, unwilling stare. Her husband was QUITE unaware of anything but his own white identity. But the Count still had a grain of secondary consciousness which hovered round and remained aware of the woman in the window-seat. The whole of his face, and his forward-looking attention was concentrated on Basil. But somewhere at the back of him he kept track of Daphne. She sat uneasy, in discontent, as women always do sit when men are locked together in a combustion of words. At the same time, she followed the argument. It was curious that, while her sympathy at this moment was with the Count, it was her husband whose words she believed to be true. The contact, the emotional contact was the real thing, the so-called 'aim' was only a by-product. Even wars and cathedrals, in her mind, were only by-products. The real thing was what the warriors and cathedral-builders had had in common, as a great uniting feeling: the thing they felt for one another, and for their women in particular, of course.

'There are a great many kinds of contact, nevertheless,' said Dionys.

'Well, do you know,' said the Major, 'it seems to me there is really only one supreme contact, the contact of love. Mind you, the love may take on an infinite variety of forms. And in my opinion, no form of love is wrong, so long as it IS love, and you yourself HONOUR what you are doing. Love has an extraordinary variety of forms! And that is all that there is in life, it seems to me. But I grant you, if you deny the VARIETY of love you deny love altogether. If you try to specialize love into one set of accepted feelings, you wound the very soul of love. Love MUST be multiform, else it is just tyranny, just death.'

'But why call it all LOVE?' said the Count.

'Because it seems to me it IS love: the great power that draws human beings together, no matter what the result of the contact may be. Of course there is hate, but hate is only the recoil of love.'

'Do you think the old Egypt was established on love?' asked Dionys.

'Why, of course! And perhaps the most multiform, the most comprehensive love that the world has seen. All that we suffer from now is that our way of love is narrow, exclusive, and therefore not love at all; more like death and tyranny.'

The Count slowly shook his head, smiling slowly and as if sadly.

'No,' he said. 'No. It is no good. You must use another word than love.'

'I don't agree at all,' said Basil.

'What word then?' blurted Daphne.

The Count looked at her.

'Obedience, submission, faith, belief, responsibility, power,' he said slowly, picking out the words slowly, as if searching for what he wanted, and never quite finding it. He looked with his quiet dark eyes into her eyes. It was curious, she disliked his words intensely, but she liked him. On the other hand, she believed absolutely what her husband said, yet her physical sympathy was against him.

'Do you agree, Daphne?' asked Basil.

'Not a bit,' she replied, with a heavy look at her husband.

'Nor I,' said Basil. 'It seems to me, if you love, there is no obedience nor submission, except to the soul of love. If you mean obedience, submission, and all the rest, to the soul of love itself, I quite agree. But if you mean obedience, submission of one person to another, and one man having power over others — I don't agree, and never shall. It seems to me just there where we have gone wrong. Kaiser Wilhelm II wanted power — '

'No, no,' said the Count. 'He was a mountebank. He had no conception of the sacredness of power.'

'He proved himself very dangerous.'

'Oh yes. But peace can be even more dangerous still.'

'Tell me, then. Do you believe that you, as an aristocrat, should have feudal power over a few hundreds of other men, who happen to be born serfs, or not aristocrats?'

'Not as a hereditary aristocrat, but as a MAN who is by nature an aristocrat,' said the Count, 'it is my sacred duty to hold the lives of other men in my hands, and to shape the issue. But I can never fulfil my destiny till men will willingly put their lives in my hands.'

'You don't expect them to, do you?' smiled Basil.

'At this moment, no.'

'Or at any moment!' The Major was sarcastic.

'At a certain moment the men who are really living will come beseeching to put their lives into the hands of the greater men among them, beseeching the greater men to take the sacred responsibility of power.'

46

'Do you think so? Perhaps you mean men will at last begin to choose leaders whom they will LOVE,' said Basil. 'I wish they would.'

'No, I mean that they will at last yield themselves before men who are greater than they: become vassals by choice.'

'Vassals!' exclaimed Basil, smiling. 'You are still in the feudal ages, Count.'

'Vassals. Not to any hereditary aristocrat — Hohenzollern or Hapsburg or Psanek,' smiled the Count. 'But to the man whose soul is born single, able to be alone, to choose and to command. At last the masses will come to such men and say: "You are greater than we. Be our lords. Take our life and our death in your hands, and dispose of us according to your will. Because we see a light in your face, and burning on your mouth."'

The Major smiled for many moments, really piqued and amused, watching the Count, who did not turn a hair.

'I say, you must be awfully naive, Count, if you believe the modern masses are ever going to behave like that. I assure you, they never will.'

'If they did,' said the Count, 'would you call it a new reign of love, or something else?'

'Well, of course, it would contain an element of love. There would have to be an element of love in their feeling for their leaders.'

'Do you think so? I thought that love assumed an equality in difference. I thought that love gave to every man the right to judge the acts of other men — "This was not an act of love, therefore it was wrong." Does not democracy, and love, give to every man this right?'

'Certainly,' said Basil.

'Ah, but my chosen aristocrat would say to those who chose him: "If you choose me, you give up forever your right to judge me. If you have truly chosen to follow me, you have thereby rejected all your right to criticize me. You can no longer either approve or disapprove of me. You have performed the sacred act of choice. Henceforth you can only obey."'

'They wouldn't be able to help criticizing, for all that,' said Daphne, blurting in her say.

He looked at her slowly, and for the first time in her life she was doubtful of what she was saying.

'The day of Judas,' he said, 'ends with the day of love.'

47

Basil woke up from a sort of trance.

'I think, of course, Count,' he said, 'that it's an awfully amusing idea. A retrogression slap back to the Dark Ages.'

'Not so,' said the Count. 'Men — the mass of men — were never before free to perform the sacred act of choice. Today — soon — they may be free.'

'Oh, I don't know. Many tribes chose their kings and chiefs.'

'Men have never before been quite free to choose: and to know what they are doing.'

'You mean they've only made themselves free in order voluntarily to saddle themselves with new lords and masters?'

'I do mean that.'

'In short, life is just a vicious circle?'

'Not at all. An ever-widening circle, as you say. Always more wonderful.'

'Well, it's all frightfully interesting and amusing — don't you think so, Daphne? By the way, Count, where would women be? Would they be allowed to criticize their husbands?'

'Only before marriage,' smiled the Count. 'Not after.'

'Splendid!' said Basil. 'I'm all for that bit of your scheme, Count. I hope you're listening, Daphne.'

'Oh yes. But then I've only married YOU, I've got my right to criticize all the other men,' she said in a dull, angry voice.

'Exactly. Clever of you! So the Count won't get off! Well now, what do you think of the Count's aristocratic scheme for the future, Daphne? Do you approve?'

'Not at all. But then little men have always wanted power,' she said cruelly.

'Oh, big men as well, for that matter,' said Basil, conciliatory.

'I have been told before,' smiled the Count, 'little men are always bossy. I am afraid I have offended Lady Daphne?'

'No,' she said. 'Not really. I'm amused, really. But I always dislike any suggestion of bullying.'

'Indeed, so do I,' said he.

'The Count didn't mean bullying, Daphne,' said Basil. 'Come, there is really an allowable distinction between responsible power and bullying.'

'When men put their heads together about it,' said she.

She was haughty and angry, as if she were afraid of losing something. The Count smiled mischievously at her.

'You are offended, Lady Daphne? But why? You are safe from any spark of my dangerous and extensive authority.'

Basil burst into a roar of laughter.

'It IS rather funny, you to be talking of power and of not being criticized,' he said. 'But I should like to hear more: I would like to hear more.'

As they drove home, he said to his wife:

'You know I like that little man. He's a quaint little bantam. And he sets one thinking.'

Lady Daphne froze to four degrees below zero, under the north wind of this statement, and not another word was to be thawed out of her.

Curiously enough, it was now Basil who was attracted by the Count, and Daphne who was repelled. Not that she was so bound up in her husband. Not at all. She was feeling rather sore against men altogether. But as so often happens, in this life based on the wicked triangle, Basil could only follow his enthusiasm for the Count in his wife's presence. When the two men were alone together, they were awkward, resistant, they could hardly get out a dozen words to one another. When Daphne was there, however, to complete the circuit of the opposing currents, things went like a house on fire.

This, however, was not much consolation to Lady Daphne. Merely to sit as a passive medium between two men who are squibbing philosophical nonsense to one another: no, it was not good enough! She almost hated the Count: low-browed little fellow, belonging to the race of prehistoric slaves. But her grudge against her white-faced, spiritually intense husband was sharp as vinegar. Let down: she was let down between the pair of them.

What next? Well, what followed was entirely Basil's fault. The winter was passing: it was obvious the war was really over, that Germany was finished. The Hohenzollern had fizzled out like a very poor squib, the Hapsburg was popping feebly in obscurity, the Romanov was smudged out without a sputter. So much for imperial royalty. Henceforth democratic peace.

The Count, of course, would be shipped back now like returned goods that had no market any more. There was a world peace ahead. A week or two, and Voynich Hall would be empty.

Basil, however, could not let matters follow their simple course. He was awfully intrigued by the Count. He wanted to entertain him as a guest before he went. And Major Apsley could get anything in reason, at this moment. So he obtained permission for the poor little Count to stay a fortnight at Thoresway, before being shipped back to Austria. Earl Beveridge, whose soul was black as ink since the war, would never have allowed the little alien enemy to enter his house, had it not been for the hatred which had been aroused in him, during the last two years, by the degrading spectacle of the so-called patriots who had been howling their mongrel indecency in the public face. These mongrels had held the Press and the British public in abeyance for almost two years. Their one aim was to degrade and humiliate anything that was proud or dignified remaining in England. It was almost the worst nightmare of all, this coming to the top of a lot of public filth which was determined to suffocate the souls of all dignified men.

Hence, the Earl, who never intended to be swamped by unclean scum, whatever else happened to him, stamped his heels in the ground and stood on his own feet. When Basil said to him, would he allow the Count to have a fortnight's decent peace in Thoresway before all was finished, Lord Beveridge gave a slow consent, scandal or no scandal. Indeed, it was really to defy scandal that he took such a step. For the thought of his dead boys was bitter to him: and the thought of England fallen under the paws of smelly mongrels was bitterer still.

Lord Beveridge was at Thoresway to receive the Count, who arrived escorted by Basil. The English Earl was a big, handsome man, rather heavy, with a dark, sombre face that would have been haughty if haughtiness had not been made so ridiculous. He was a passionate man, with a passionate man's sensitiveness, generosity, and instinctive overbearing. But HIS dark passionate nature, and his violent sensitiveness had been subjected now to fifty-five years' subtle repression, condemnation, repudiation, till he had almost come to believe in his own wrongness. His little, frail wife, all love for humanity, she was the genuine article. Himself, he was labelled selfish, sensual, cruel, etc., etc. So by now he always seemed to be standing aside, in the shadow, letting himself be obliterated by the pallid rabble of the democratic hurry. That was the impression he gave of a man standing back, half-ashamed, half-haughty, semi-hidden in the dark background.

He was a little on the defensive as Basil came in with the Count.

'Ah — how do you do, Count Psanek?' he said, striding largely forward and holding out his hand. Because he was the father of Daphne the Count felt a certain tenderness for the taciturn Englishman.

'You do me too much honour, my lord, receiving me in your house,' said the small Count proudly.

The Earl looked at him slowly, without speaking: seemed to look down on him, in every sense of the words.

'We are still men, Count. We are not beasts altogether.'

'You wish to say that my countrymen are so very nearly beasts, Lord Beveridge?' smiled the Count, curling his fine nose.

Again the Earl was slow in replying.

'You have a low opinion of my manners, Count Psanek.'

'But perhaps a just appreciation of your meaning, Lord Beveridge,' smiled the Count, with the same reckless little look of contempt on his nose.

Lord Beveridge flushed dark, with all his native anger offended.

'I am glad Count Psanek makes my own meaning clear to me,' he said.

'I beg your pardon a thousand times, my lord, if I give offence in doing so,' replied the Count.

The Earl went black, and felt a fool. He turned his back on the Count. And then he turned round again, offering his cigar-case.

'Will you smoke?' he said. There was kindness in his tone.

'Thank you,' said the Count, taking a cigar.

'I dare say,' said Lord Beveridge, 'that all men are beasts in some way. I am afraid I have fallen into the common habit of speaking by rote, and not what I really mean. Won't you take a seat?'

'It is only as a prisoner that I have learned that I am NOT truly a beast. No, I am myself. I am not a beast,' said the Count, seating himself.

The Earl eyed him curiously.

'Well,' he said, smiling, 'I suppose it is best to come to a decision about it.'

51

'It is necessary, if one is to be safe from vulgarity.'

The Earl felt a twinge of accusation. With his agate-brown, hard-looking eyes he watched the black-browed little Count.

'You are probably right,' he said.

But he turned his face aside.

They were five people at dinner — Lady Beveridge was there as hostess.

'Ah, Count Dionys,' she said with a sigh, 'do you really feel that the war is over?'

'Oh yes,' he replied quickly. 'This war is over. The armies will go home. THEIR cannon will not sound any more. Never again like this.'

'Ah, I hope so,' she sighed.

'I am sure,' he said.

'You think there'll be no more war?' said Daphne.

For some reason she had made herself very fine, in her newest dress of silver and black and pink-chenille, with bare shoulders, and her hair fashionably done. The Count in his shabby uniform turned to her. She was nervous, hurried. Her slim white arm was near him, with the bit of silver at the shoulder. Her skin was white like a hot-house flower. Her lips moved hurriedly.

'Such a war as this there will never be again,' he said.

'What makes you so sure?' she replied, glancing into his eyes.

'The machine of war has got out of our control. We shall never start it again, till it has fallen to pieces. We shall be afraid.'

'Will everybody be afraid?' said she, looking down and pressing back her chin.

'I think so.'

'We will hope so,' said Lady Beveridge.

'Do you mind if I ask you, Count,' said Basil, 'what you feel about the way the war has ended? The way it has ended for YOU, I mean.'

'You mean that Germany and Austria have lost the war? It was bound to be. We have all lost the war. All Europe.'

'I agreee there,' said Lord Beveridge.

'We've all lost the war?' said Daphne, turning to look at him.

There was pain on his dark, low-browed face. He suffered having the sensitive woman beside him. Her skin had a hothouse delicacy that made his head go round. Her shoulders were broad, rather thin, but the skin was white and so sensitive, so hot-house delicate. It affected him like the perfume of some white, exotic flower. And she seemed to be sending her heart towards him. It was as if she wanted to press her breast to his. From the breast she loved him, and sent out love to him. And it made him unhappy; he wanted to be quiet, and to keep his honour before these hosts.

He looked into her eyes, his own eyes dark with knowledge and pain. She, in her silence and her brief words seemed to be holding them all under her spell. She seemed to have cast a certain muteness on the table, in the midst of which she remained silently master, leaning forward to her plate, and silently mastering them all.

'Don't I think we've all lost the war?' he replied, in answer to her question. 'It was a war of suicide. Nobody could win it. It was suicide for all of us.'

'Oh, I don't know,' she replied. 'What about America and Japan?'

'They don't count. They only helped US to commit suicide. They did not enter vitally.'

There was such a look of pain on his face, and such a sound of pain in his voice, that the other three closed their ears, shut off from attending. Only Daphne was making him speak. It was she who was drawing the soul out of him, trying to read the future in him as the augurs read the future in the quivering entrails of the sacrificed beast. She looked direct into his face, searching his soul.

'You think Europe has committed suicide?' she said.

'Morally.'

'Only morally?' came her slow, bronze-like words, so fatal.

'That is enough,' he smiled.

'Quite,' she said, with a slow droop of her eyelids. Then she turned away her face. But he felt the heart strangling inside his breast. What was she doing now? What was she thinking? She filled him with uncertainty and with uncanny fear.

'At least,' said Basil, 'those infernal guns are quiet.'

'For ever,' said Dionys.

'I wish I could believe you, Count,' said the Major.

The talk became more general — or more personal. Lady Beveridge asked Dionys about his wife and family. He knew nothing save that they had gone to Hungary in 1916, when his own house was burnt down. His wife might even have gone to Bulgaria with Prince Bogorik. He did not know.

'But your children, Count!' cried Lady Beveridge.

'I do not know. Probably in Hungary, with their grandmother. I will go when I get back.'

'But have you never WRITTEN? — never inquired?'

'I could not write. I shall know soon enough — everything.'

'You have no son?'

'No. Two girls.'

'Poor things!'

'Yes.'

'I say, isn't it an odd thing to have a ladybird on your crest?' asked Basil, to cheer up the conversation.

'Why queer? Charlemagne had bees. And it is a Marienkafer — a Mary-beetle. The beetle of Our Lady. I think it is quite a heraldic insect, Major,' smiled the Count.

'You're proud of it?' said Daphne, suddenly turning to look at him again, with her slow, pregnant look.

'I am, you know. It has such a long genealogy — our spotted beetle. Much longer than the Psaneks. I think, you know, it is a descendant of the Egyptian scarabeus, which is a very mysterious emblem. So I connect myself with the Pharaohs: just through my ladybird.'

'You feel your ladybird has crept through so many ages,' she said.

'Imagine it!' he laughed.

'The scarab IS a piquant insect,' said Basil.

'Do you know Fabre?' put in Lord Beveridge. 'He suggests that the beetle rolling a little ball of dung before him, in a dry old field, must have suggested to the Egyptians the First Principle that set the globe rolling. And so the scarab became the symbol of the creative principle — or something like that.'

'That the earth is a tiny ball of dry dung is good,' said Basil.

'Between the claws of a ladybird,' added Daphne.

'That is what it is, to go back to one's origin,' said Lady Beveridge.

'Perhaps they meant that it was the principle of decomposition which first set the ball rolling,' said the Count.

'The ball would have to be THERE first,' said Basil.

'Certainly. But it hadn't started to roll. Then the principle of decomposition started it.' The Count smiled as if it were a joke.

54

'I am no Egyptologist,' said Lady Beveridge, 'so I can't judge.'

The Earl and Countess Beveridge left next day. Count Dionys was left with the two young people in the house. It was a beautiful Elizabethan mansion, not very large, but with those magical rooms that are all a twinkle of small-paned windows, looking out from the dark panelled interior. The interior was cosy, panelled to the ceiling, and the ceiling moulded and touched with gold. And then the great square bow of the window with its little panes intervening like magic between oneself and the world outside, the crest in stained glass crowning its colour, the broad window-seat cushioned in faded green. Dionys wandered round the house like a little ghost, through the succession of small and large twinkling sitting-rooms and lounge rooms in front, down the long, wide corridor with the wide stairhead at each end, and up the narrow stairs to the bedrooms above, and on to the roof.

It was early spring, and he loved to sit on the leaded, pale-grey roof that had its queer seats and slopes, a little pale world in itself. Then to look down over the garden and the sloping lawn to the ponds massed round with trees, and away to the elms and furrows and hedges of the shires. On the left of the house was the farmstead, with ricks and great-roofed barns and dark-red cattle. Away to the right, beyond the park, was a village among trees, and the spark of a grey church spire.

He liked to be alone, feeling his soul heavy with its own fate. He would sit for hours watching the elm trees standing in rows like giants, like warriors across the country. The Earl had told him that the Romans had brought these elms to Britain. And he seemed to see the spirit of the Romans in them still. Sitting there alone in the spring sunshine, in the solitude of the roof, he saw the glamour of this England of hedgerows and elm trees, and the labourers with slow horses slowly drilling the sod, crossing the brown furrow: and the roofs of the village, with the church steeple rising beside a big black yew tree: and the chequer of fields away to the distance.

And the charm of the old manor around him, the garden with its grey stone walls and yew hedges — broad, broad yew hedges and a peacock pausing to glitter and scream in the busy silence of an English spring, when celandines open their yellow under the hedges, and violets are in the secret, and by the broad paths of the garden polyanthus and crocuses vary the velvet and flame, and bits of yellow wallflower shake raggedly, with a wonderful triumphance, out of the cracks of the wall. There was a fold somewhere near, and he could hear the treble bleat of the growing lambs, and the deeper, contented baaing of the ewes.

This was Daphne's home, where she had been born. She loved it with an ache of affection. But now it was hard to forget her dead brothers. She wandered about in the sun, with two old dogs padding after her. She talked with everybody — gardener, groom, stableman, with the farm-hands. That filled a large part of her life — straying round talking with the work-people. They were, of course, respectful to her — but not at all afraid of her. They knew she was poor, that she could not afford a car, nor anything. So they talked to her very freely: perhaps a little too freely. Yet she let it be. It was her one passion at Thoresway to hear the dependants talk and talk — about everything. The curious feeling of intimacy across a breach fascinated her. Their lives fascinated her: what they thought, what they FELT. These, what they felt. That fascinated her. There was a gamekeeper she could have loved — an impudent, ruddy-faced, laughing, ingratiating fellow; she could have loved him, if he had not been isolated beyond the breach of his birth, her culture, her consciousness. Her CONSCIOUSNESS seemed to make a great gulf between her and the lower classes, the unconscious classes. She accepted it as her doom. She could never meet in real contact anyone but a super-conscious, finished being like herself: or like her husband. Her father had some of the unconscious blood-warmth of the lower classes. But he was like a man who is damned. And the Count, of course. The Count had something that was hot and invisible, a dark flame of life that might warm the cold white fire of her own blood. But —

They avoided each other. All three, they avoided one another. Basil, too, went off alone. Or he immersed himself in poetry. Sometimes he and the Count played billiards. Sometimes all three walked in the park. Often Basil and Daphne walked to the village, to post. But truly, they avoided one another, all three. The days slipped by.

At evening they sat together in the small west room that had books and a piano and comfortable shabby furniture of faded rose-coloured tapestry: a shabby room. Sometimes Basil read aloud: sometimes the Count played the piano. And they talked. And Daphne stitch by stitch went on with a big embroidered bedspread, which she might finish if she lived long enough. But they always went to bed early. They were nearly always avoiding one another.

Dionys had a bedroom in the east bay — a long way from the rooms of the others. He had a habit, when he was quite alone, of singing, or rather crooning, to himself the old songs of his childhood. It was only when he felt he was quite alone: when other people seemed to fade out of him, and all the world seemed to dissolve into darkness, and there was nothing but himself, his own soul, alive in the middle of his own small night, isolate for ever. Then, half unconscious, he would croon in a small, high-pitched, squeezed voice, a sort of high dream-voice, the songs of his childhood dialect. It was a curious noise: the sound of a man who is alone in his own blood: almost the sound of a man who is going to be executed.

Daphne heard the sound one night when she was going downstairs again with the corridor lantern to find a book. She was a bad sleeper, and her nights were a torture to her. She, too, like a neurotic, was nailed inside her own fretful self-consciousness. But she had a very keen ear. So she started as she heard the small, bat-like sound of the Count's singing to himself. She stood in the midst of the wide corridor, that was wide as a room, carpeted with a faded lavender-coloured carpet, with a piece of massive dark furniture at intervals by the wall, and an oak arm-chair and sometimes a faded, reddish Oriental rug. The big horn lantern which stood at nights at the end of the corridor she held in her hand. The intense 'peeping' sound of the Count, like a witchcraft, made her forget everything. She could not understand a word, of course. She could not understand the noise even. After listening for a long time, she went on downstairs. When she came back again he was still, and the light was gone from under his door.

After this, it became almost an obsession to her to listen for him. She waited with fretful impatience for ten o'clock, when she could retire. She waited more fretfully still for the maid to leave her, and for her husband to come and say good-night. Basil had the room across the corridor. And then in resentful impatience she waited for the sounds of the house to become still. Then she opened her door to listen.

And far away, as if from far, far away in the unseen, like a ventriloquist sound or a bat's uncanny peeping, came the frail, almost inaudible sound of the Count's singing to himself before he went to bed. It WAS inaudible to anyone but herself. But she, by concentration, seemed to hear supernaturally. She had a low arm-chair by the door, and there, wrapped in a huge old black silk shawl, she sat and listened. At first she could not hear. That is, she could hear the sound. But it was only a sound. And then, gradually, gradually she began to follow the thread of it. It was like a thread which she followed out of the world: out of the world. And as she went, slowly, by degrees, far, far away, down the thin thread of his singing, she knew peace — she knew forgetfulness. She could pass beyond the world, away beyond where her soul balanced like a bird on wings, and was perfected.

So it was, in her upper spirit. But underneath was a wild, wild yearning, actually to go, actually to be given. Actually to go, actually to die the death, actually to cross the border and be gone, to be gone. To be gone from this herself, from this Daphne, to be gone from father and mother, brothers and husband, and home and land and world: to be gone. To be gone to the call from the beyond: the call. It was the Count calling. He was calling her. She was sure he was calling her. Out of herself, out of her world, he was calling her.

Two nights she sat just inside her room, by the open door, and listened. Then when he finished she went to sleep, a queer, light, bewitched sleep. In the day she was bewitched. She felt strange and light, as if pressure had been removed from around her. Some pressure had been clamped round her all her life. She had never realized it till now; now it was removed, and her feet felt so light, and her breathing delicate and exquisite. There had always been a pressure against her breathing. Now she breathed delicate and exquisite, so that it was a delight to breathe. Life came in exquisite breaths, quickly, as if it delighted to come to her.

The third night he was silent — though she waited and waited till the small hours of the morning. He was silent, he did not sing. And then she knew the terror and blackness of the feeling that he might never sing any more. She waited like one doomed, throughout the day. And when the night came she trembled. It was her greatest nervous terror, lest her spell should be broken, and she should be thrown back to what she was before.

Night came, and the kind of swoon upon her. Yes, and the call from the night. The call! She rose helplessly and hurried down the corridor. The light was under his door. She sat down in the big oak arm-chair that stood near his door, and huddled herself tight in her black shawl. The corridor was dim with the big, star-studded, yellow lantern-light. Away down she could see the lamp-light in her doorway; she had left her door ajar.

But she saw nothing. Only she wrapped herself close in the black shawl, and listened to the sound from the room. It called. Oh, it called her! Why could she not go? Why could she not cross through the closed door.

Then the noise ceased. And then the light went out, under the door of his room. Must she go back? Must she go back? Oh, impossible. As impossible as that the moon should go back on her tracks, once she has risen. Daphne sat on, wrapped in her black shawl. If it must be so, she would sit on through eternity. Return she never could.

And then began the most terrible song of all. It began with a rather dreary, slow, horrible sound, like death. And then suddenly came a real call — fluty, and a kind of whistling and a strange whirr at the changes, most imperative, and utterly inhuman. Daphne rose to her feet. And at the same moment up rose the whistling throb of a summons out of the death moan.

Daphne tapped low and rapidly at the door. 'Count! Count!' she whispered. The sound inside ceased. The door suddenly opened. The pale, obscure figure of Dionys.

'Lady Daphne!' he said in astonishment, automatically standing aside.

'You called,' she murmured rapidly, and she passed intent into his room.

'No, I did not call,' he said gently, his hand on the door still.

'Shut the door,' she said abruptly.

He did as he was bid. The room was in complete darkness. There was no moon outside. She could not see him.

'Where can I sit down?' she said abruptly.

'I will take you to the couch,' he said, putting out his hand and touching her in the dark. She shuddered.

She found the couch and sat down. It was quite dark.

'What are you singing?' she said rapidly.

'I am so sorry. I did not think anyone could hear.'

'What was it you were singing?'

'A song of my country.'

'Had it any words?'

'Yes, it is a woman who was a swan, and who loved a hunter by the marsh. So she became a woman and married him and had three children. Then in the night one night the king of the swans called to her to come back, or else he would die. So slowly she turned into a swan again, and slowly she opened her wide, wide wings, and left her husband and her children.'

There was silence in the dark room. The Count had been really startled, startled out of his mood of the song into the day-mood of human convention. He was distressed and embarrassed by Daphne's presence in his dark room. She, however, sat on and did not make a sound. He, too, sat down in a chair by the window. It was everywhere dark. A wind was blowing in gusts outside. He could see nothing inside his room: only the faint, faint strip of light under the door. But he could feel her presence in the darkness. It was uncanny, to feel her near in the dark, and not to see any sign of her, nor to hear any sound.

She had been wounded in her bewitched state by the contact with the every-day human being in him. But now she began to relapse into her spell, as she sat there in the dark. And he, too, in the silence, felt the world sinking away from him once more, leaving him once more alone on a darkened earth, with nothing between him and the infinite dark space. Except now her presence. Darkness answering to darkness, and deep answering to deep. An answer, near to him, and invisible.

But he did not know what to do. He sat still and silent as she was still and silent. The darkness inside the room seemed alive like blood. He had no power to move. The distance between them seemed absolute.

Then suddenly, without knowing, he went across in the dark, feeling for the end of the couch. And he sat beside her on the couch. But he did not touch her. Neither did she move. The darkness flowed about them thick like blood, and time seemed dissolved in it. They sat with the small, invisible distance between them, motionless, speechless, thoughtless.

Then suddenly he felt her finger-tips touch his arm, and a flame

60

went over him that left him no more a man. He was something seated in flame, in flame unconscious, seated erect, like an Egyptian King-god in the statues. Her finger-tips slid down him, and she herself slid down in a strange, silent rush, and he felt her face against his closed feet and ankles, her hands pressing his ankles. He felt her brow and hair against his ankles, her face against his feet, and there she clung in the dark, as if in space below him. He still sat erect and motionless. Then he bent forward and put his hand on her hair.

'Do you come to me?' he murmured. 'Do you come to me?'

The flame that enveloped him seemed to sway him silently.

'Do you really come to me?' he repeated. 'But we have nowhere to go.'

He felt his bare feet wet with her tears. Two things were struggling in him, the sense of eternal solitude, like space, and the rush of dark flame that would throw him out of his solitude towards her.

He was thinking too. He was thinking of the future. He had no future in the world: of that he was conscious. He had no future in this life. Even if he lived on, it would only be a kind of enduring. But he felt that in the after-life the inheritance was his. He felt the after-life belonged to him.

Future in the world he could not give her. Life in the world he had not to offer her. Better go on alone. Surely better go on alone.

But then the tears on his feet: and her face that would face him as he left her! No, no. The next life was his. He was master of the after-life. Why fear for this life? Why not take the soul she offered him? Now and for ever, for the life that would come when they both were dead. Take her into the underworld. Take her into the dark Hades with him, like Francesca and Paolo. And in hell hold her fast, queen of the underworld, himself master of the underworld. Master of the life to come. Father of the soul that would come after.

'Listen,' he said to her softly. 'Now you are mine. In the dark you are mine. And when you die you are mine. But in the day you are not mine, because I have no power in the day. In the night, in the dark, and in death, you are mine. And that is for ever. No matter if I must leave you. I shall come again from time to time. In the dark you are mine. But in the day I cannot claim you. I have no power in the day, and no place. So remember. When the darkness comes, I shall always be in the darkness of you. And as long as I live, from time to time I shall come to find you, when I am able to, when I am not a prisoner. But I shall have to go away soon. So don't forget — you are the night wife of the ladybird, while you live and even when you die.'

Later, when he took her back to her room, he saw the door still ajar.

'You shouldn't leave a light in your room,' he murmured.

In the morning there was a curious remote look about him. He was quieter than ever, and seemed very far away. Daphne slept late. She had a strange feeling as if she had slipped off all her cares. She did not care, she did not grieve, she did not fret any more. All that had left her. She felt she could sleep, sleep, sleep — for ever. Her face, too, was very still, with a delicate look of virginity that she had never had before. She had always been Aphrodite, the self-conscious one. And her eyes, the green-blue, had been like slow, living jewels, resistant. Now they had unfolded from the hard flower-bud, and had the wonder, and the stillness of a quiet night.

Basil noticed it at once.

'You're different, Daphne,' he said. 'What are you thinking about?'

'I wasn't thinking,' she said, looking at him with candour.

'What were you doing then?'

'What does one do when one doesn't think? Don't make me puzzle it out, Basil.'

'Not a bit of it, if you don't want to.'

But he was puzzled by her. The sting of his ecstatic love for her seemed to have left him. Yet he did not know what else to do but to make love to her. She went very pale. She submitted to him, bowing her head because she was his wife. But she looked at him with fear, with sorrow, with real suffering. He could feel the heaving of her breast, and knew she was weeping. But there were no tears on her face, she was only death pale. Her eyes were shut.

'Are you in pain?' he asked her.

'No! no!' She opened her eyes, afraid lest she had disturbed him. She did not want to disturb him.

He was puzzled. His own ecstatic, deadly love for her had received a check. He was out of the reckoning.

He watched her when she was with the Count. Then she seemed so meek — so maidenly — so different from what he had known of her.

62

She was so still, like a virgin girl. And it was this quiet, intact quality of Virginity in her which puzzled him most, puzzled his emotions and his ideas. He became suddenly ashamed to make love to her. And because he was ashamed, he said to her as he stood in her room that night:

'Daphne, are you in love with the Count?'

He was standing by the dressing-table, uneasy. She was seated in a low chair by the tiny dying wood fire. She looked up at him with wide, slow eyes. Without a word, with wide, soft, dilated eyes she watched him. What was it that made him feel all confused? He turned his face aside, away from her wide, soft eyes.

'Pardon me, dear. I didn't intend to ask such a question. Don't take any notice of it,' he said. And he strode away and picked up a book. She lowered her head and gazed abstractedly into the fire, without a sound. Then he looked at her again, at her bright hair that the maid had plaited for the night. Her plait hung down over her soft pinkish wrap. His heart softened to her as he saw her sitting there. She seemed like his sister. The excitement of desire had left him, and now he seemed to see clear and feel true for the first time in his life. She was like a dear, dear sister to him. He felt that she was his blood-sister, nearer to him than he had imagined any woman could be. So near — so dear — and all the sex and the desire gone. He didn't want it — he hadn't wanted it. This new pure feeling was so much more wonderful.

He went to her side.

'Forgive me, darling,' he said, 'for having questioned you.'

She looked up at him with the wide eyes, without a word. His face was good and beautiful. Tears came to her eyes.

'You have the right to question me,' she said sadly.

'No,' he said. 'No, darling. I have no right to question you. Daphne! Daphne, darling! It shall be as YOU wish, between us. Shall it? Shall it be as you wish?'

'You are the husband, Basil,' she said sadly.

'Yes, darling. But' — he went on his knees beside her — 'perhaps, darling, something has changed in us. I feel as if I ought never to touch you again — as if I never WANTED to touch you — in that way. I feel it was wrong, darling. Tell me what you think.' 'Basil, don't be angry with me.'

'It isn't anger; it's pure love, darling — it is.'

63

'Let us not come any nearer to one another than this, Basil — physically — shall we?' she said. 'And don't be angry with me, will you?'

'Why,' he said. 'I think myself the sexual part has been a mistake. I had rather love you — as I love now. I KNOW that this is true love. The other was always a bit whipped up. I KNOW I love you now, darling: now I'm free from that other. But what if it comes upon me, that other, Daphne?'

'I am always your wife,' she said quietly. 'I am always your wife. I want always to obey you, Basil: what you wish.'

'Give me your hand, dear.'

She gave him her hand. But the look in her eyes at the same time warned him and frightened him. He kissed her hand and left her.

It was to the Count she belonged. This had decided itself in her down to the depths of her soul. If she could not marry him and be his wife in the world, it had nevertheless happened to her for ever. She could no more question it. Question had gone out of her.

Strange how different she had become — a strange new quiescence. The last days were slipping past. He would be going away — Dionys: he with the still remote face, the man she belonged to in the dark and in the light, for ever. He would be going away. He said it must be so. And she acquiesced. The grief was deep, deep inside her. He must go away. Their lives could not be one life, in this world's day. Even in her anguish she knew it was so. She knew he was right. He was for her infallible. He spoke the deepest soul in her.

She never SAW him as a lover. When she saw him, he was the little officer, a prisoner, quiet, claiming nothing in all the world. And when she went to him as his lover, his wife, it was always dark. She only knew his voice and his contact in darkness. 'My wife in darkness,' he said to her. And in this too she believed him. She would not have contradicted him, no, not for anything on earth: lest contradicting him she should lose the dark treasures of stillness and bliss which she kept in her breast even when her heart was wrung with the agony of knowing he must go.

No, she had found this wonderful thing after she had heard him singing: she had suddenly collapsed away from her old self into this darkness, this peace, this quiescence that was like a full dark river flowing eternally in her soul. She had gone to sleep from the nuit blanche of her days. And Basil, wonderful, had changed almost at once. She feared him, lest he might change back again. She would always have him to fear. But deep inside her she only feared for this love of hers for the Count: this dark, everlasting love that was like a full river flowing for ever inside her. Ah, let that not be broken.

She was so still inside her. She could sit so still, and feel the day slowly, richly changing to night. And she wanted nothing, she was short of nothing. If only Dionys need not go away! If only he need not go away!

But he said to her, the last morning:

'Don't forget me. Always remember me. I leave my soul in your hands and your womb. Nothing can ever separate us, unless we betray one another. If you have to give yourself to your husband, do so, and obey him. If you are true to me, innerly, innerly true, he will not hurt us. He is generous, be generous to him. And never fail to believe in me. Because even on the other side of death I shall be watching for you. I shall be king in Hades when I am dead. And you will be at my side. You will never leave me any more, in the after-death. So don't be afraid in life. Don't be afraid. If you have to cry tears, cry them. But in your heart of hearts know that I shall come again, and that I have taken you for ever. And so, in your heart of hearts be still, be still, since you are the wife of the ladybird.' He laughed as he left her, with his own beautiful, fearless laugh. But they were strange eyes that looked after him.

He went in the car with Basil back to Voynich Hall.

'I believe Daphne will miss you,' said Basil.

The Count did not reply for some moments.

'Well, if she does,' he said, 'there will be no bitterness in it.'

'Are you sure?' smiled Basil.

'Why — if we are sure of anything,' smiled the Count.

'She's changed, isn't she?'

'Is she?'

'Yes, she's quite changed since you came, Count.'

'She does not seem to me so very different from the girl of seventeen whom I knew.'

'No — perhaps not. I didn't know her then. But she's very different from the wife I have known.'

'A regrettable difference?'

'Well — no, not as far as she goes. She is much quieter inside herself. You know, Count, something of me died in the war. I feel it will take me an eternity to sit and think about it all.'

'I hope you may think it out to your satisfaction, Major.'

'Yes, I hope so too. But that is how it has left me — feeling as if I needed eternity now to brood about it all, you know. Without the need to act — or even to love, really. I suppose love is action.'

'Intense action,' said the Count.

'Quite so. I know really how I feel. I only ask of life to spare me from further effort of action of any sort — even love. And then to fulfil myself, brooding through eternity. Of course, I don't mind WORK, mechanical action. That in itself is a form of inaction.'

'A man can only be happy following his own inmost need,' said the Count.

'Exactly!' said Basil. 'I will lay down the law for nobody, not even for myself. And live my day — '

'Then you will be happy in your own way. I find it so difficult to keep from laying the law down for myself,' said the Count. 'Only the thought of death and the after life saves me from doing it any more.'

'As the thought of eternity helps me,' said Basil. 'I suppose it amounts to the same thing.'

The Fox

The two girls were usually known by their surnames, Banford and March. They had taken the farm together, intending to work it all by themselves: that is, they were going to rear chickens, make a living by poultry, and add to this by keeping a cow, and raising one or two young beasts. Unfortunately, things did not turn out well.

Banford was a small, thin, delicate thing with spectacles. She, however, was the principal investor, for March had little or no money. Banford's father, who was a tradesman in Islington, gave his daughter the start, for her health's sake, and because he loved her, and because it did not look as if she would marry. March was more robust. She had learned carpentry and joinery at the evening classes in Islington. She would be the man about the place. They had, moreover, Banford's old grandfather living with them at the start. He had been a farmer. But unfortunately the old man died after he had been at Bailey Farm for a year. Then the two girls were left alone.

They were neither of them young: that is, they were near thirty. But they certainly were not old. They set out quite gallantly with their enterprise. They had numbers of chickens, black Leghorns and white Leghorns, Plymouths and Wyandottes; also some ducks; also two heifers in the fields. One heifer, unfortunately, refused absolutely to stay in the Bailey Farm closes. No matter how March made up the fences, the heifer was out, wild in the woods, or trespassing on the neighbouring pasture, and March and Banford were away, flying after her, with more haste than success. So this heifer they sold in despair. Then, just before the other beast was expecting her first calf, the old man died, and the girls, afraid of the coming event, sold her in a panic, and limited their attentions to fowls and ducks.

In spite of a little chagrin, it was a relief to have no more cattle on hand. Life was not made merely to be slaved away. Both girls agreed in this. The fowls were quite enough trouble. March had set up her carpenter's bench at the end of the open shed. Here she worked, making coops and doors and other appurtenances. The fowls were housed in the bigger building, which had served as barn and cow-shed in old days. They had a beautiful home, and should have been perfectly content. Indeed, they looked well enough. But the girls were disgusted at their tendency to strange illnesses, at their exacting way of life, and at their refusal, obstinate refusal to lay eggs.

March did most of the outdoor work. When she was out and about, in her puttees and breeches, her belted coat and her loose cap, she looked almost like some graceful, loose-balanced young man, for her shoulders were straight, and her movements easy and confident, even tinged with a little indifference or irony. But her face was not a man's face, ever. The wisps of her crisp dark hair blew about her as she stooped, her eyes were big and wide and dark, when she looked up again, strange, startled, shy and sardonic at once. Her mouth, too, was almost pinched as if in pain and irony. There was something odd and unexplained about her. She would stand balanced on one hip, looking at the fowls pattering about in the obnoxious fine mud of the sloping yard, and calling to her favourite white hen, which came in answer to her name. But there was an almost satirical flicker in March's big, dark eyes as she looked at her three-toed flock pottering about under her gaze, and the same slight dangerous satire in her voice as she spoke to the favoured Patty, who pecked at March's boot by way of friendly demonstration.

Fowls did not flourish at Bailey Farm, in spite of all that March did for them. When she provided hot food for them in the morning, according to rule, she noticed that it made them heavy and dozy for hours. She expected to see them lean against the pillars of the shed in their languid processes of digestion. And she knew quite well that they ought to be busily scratching and foraging about, if they were to come to any good. So she decided to give them their hot food at night, and let them sleep on it. Which she did. But it made no difference.

War conditions, again, were very unfavourable to poultry-keeping. Food was scarce and bad. And when the Daylight Saving Bill was passed, the fowls obstinately refused to go to bed as usual, about nine o'clock in the summer-time. That was late enough, indeed, for there was no peace till they were shut up and asleep. Now they cheerfully walked around, without so much as glancing at the barn, until ten o'clock or later. Both Banford and March disbelieved in living for work alone. They wanted to read or take a cycle-ride in the evening, or perhaps March wished to paint curvilinear swans on porcelain, with green background, or else make a marvellous fire-screen by processes of elaborate cabinet work. For she was a creature of odd whims and unsatisfied tendencies. But from all these things she was prevented by the stupid fowls.

One evil there was greater than any other. Bailey Farm was a little homestead, with ancient wooden barn and low-gabled farm-house, lying just one field removed from the edge of the wood. Since the war the fox was a demon. He carried off the hens under the very noses of March and Banford. Banford would start and stare through her big spectacles with all her eyes, as another squawk and flutter took place at her heels. Too late! Another white Leghorn gone. It was disheartening.

They did what they could to remedy it. When it became permitted to shoot foxes, they stood sentinel with their guns, the two of them, at the favoured hours. But it was no good. The fox was too quick for them. So another year passed, and another, and they were living on their losses, as Banford said. They let their farm-house one summer, and retired to live in a railway-carriage that was deposited as a sort of out-house in a corner of the field. This amused them, and helped their finances. None the less, things looked dark.

Although they were usually the best of friends, because Banford, though nervous and delicate, was a warm, generous soul, and March, though so odd and absent in herself, had a strange magnanimity, yet, in the long solitude, they were apt to become a little irritable with one another, tired of one another. March had four-fifths of the work to do, and though she did not mind, there seemed no relief, and it made her eyes flash curiously sometimes. Then Banford, feeling more nerve-worn than ever, would become despondent, and March would speak sharply to her. They seemed to be losing ground, somehow, losing hope as the months went by. There alone in the fields by the wood, with the wide country stretching hollow and dim to the round hills of the White Horse, in the far distance, they seemed to have to live too much off themselves. There was nothing to keep them up - and no hope.

The fox really exasperated them both. As soon as they had let the fowls out, in the early summer mornings, they had to take their guns and keep guard: and then again as soon as evening began to mellow, they must go once more. And he was so sly. He slid along in the deep grass; he was difficult as a serpent to see. And he seemed to circumvent the girls deliberately. Once or twice March had caught sight of the white tip of his brush, or the ruddy shadow of him in the deep grass, and she had let fire at him. But he made no account of this.

One evening March was standing with her back to the sunset, her gun under her arm, her hair pushed under her cap. She was half watching, half musing. It was her constant state. Her eyes were keen and observant, but her inner mind took no notice of what she saw. She was always lapsing into this odd, rapt state, her mouth rather screwed up. It was a question whether she was there, actually conscious present, or not.

The trees on the wood-edge were a darkish, brownish green in the full light - for it was the end of August. Beyond, the naked, copper-like shafts and limbs of the pine trees shone in the air. Nearer the rough grass, with its long, brownish stalks all agleam, was full of light. The fowls were round about - the ducks were still swimming on the pond under the pine trees. March looked at it all, saw it all, and did not see it. She heard Banford speaking to the fowls in the distance - and she did not hear. What was she thinking about? Heaven knows. Her consciousness was, as it were, held back.

She lowered her eyes, and suddenly saw the fox. He was looking up at her. Her chin was pressed down, and his eyes were looking up. They met her eyes. And he knew her. She was spellbound - she knew he knew her. So he looked into her eyes, and her soul failed her. He knew her, he was not daunted.

She struggled, confusedly she came to herself, and saw him making off, with slow leaps over some fallen boughs, slow, impudent jumps. Then he glanced over his shoulder, and ran smoothly away. She saw his brush held smooth like a feather, she saw his white buttocks twinkle. And he was gone, softly, soft as the wind.

She put her gun to her shoulder, but even then pursed her mouth, knowing it was nonsense to pretend to fire. So she began to walk slowly after him, in the direction he had gone, slowly, pertinaciously. She expected to find him. In her heart she was determined to find him. What she would do when she saw him again she did not consider. But she was determined to find him. So she walked abstractedly about on the edge of the wood, with wide, vivid dark eyes, and a faint flush in her cheeks. She did not think. In strange mindlessness she walked hither and thither.

At last she became aware that Banford was calling her. She made an effort of attention, turned, and gave some sort of screaming call in answer. Then again she was striding off towards the homestead. The red sun was setting, the fowls were retiring towards their roost. She watched them, white creatures, black creatures, gathering to the barn. She watched them spellbound, without seeing them. But her automatic intelligence told her when it was time to shut the door.

She went indoors to supper, which Banford had set on the table. Banford chatted easily. March seemed to listen, in her distant, manly way. She answered a brief word now and then. But all the time she was as if spellbound. And as soon as supper was over, she rose again to go out, without saying why.

She took her gun again and went to look for the fox. For he had lifted his eyes upon her, and his knowing look seemed to have entered her brain. She did not so much think of him: she was possessed by him. She saw his dark, shrewd, unabashed eye looking into her, knowing her. She felt him invisibly master her spirit. She knew the way he lowered his chin as he looked up, she knew his muzzle, the golden brown, and the greyish white. And again she saw him glance over his shoulder at her, half inviting, half contemptuous and cunning. So she went, with her great startled eyes glowing, her gun under her arm, along the wood edge. Meanwhile the night fell, and a great moon rose above the pine trees. And again Banford was calling.

So she went indoors. She was silent and busy. She examined her gun, and cleaned it, musing abstractedly by the lamplight. Then she went out again, under the great moon, to see if everything was right. When she saw the dark crests of the pine trees against the blood-red sky, again her heart beat to the fox, the fox. She wanted to follow him, with her gun.

It was some days before she mentioned the affair to Banford. Then suddenly one evening she said:

'The fox was right at my feet on Saturday night.'

'Where?' said Banford, her eyes opening behind her spectacles.

'When I stood just above the pond.'

'Did you fire?' cried Banford.

71

'No, I didn't.'

'Why not?'

'Why, I was too much surprised, I suppose.'

It was the same old, slow, laconic way of speech March always had. Banford stared at her friend for a few moments.

'You saw him?' she cried.

'Oh yes! He was looking up at me, cool as anything.'

'I tell you,' cried Banford - 'the cheek! They're not afraid of us, Nellie.'

'Oh, no,' said March.

'Pity you didn't get a shot at him,' said Banford.

'Isn't it a pity! I've been looking for him ever since. But I don't suppose he'll come so near again.'

'I don't suppose he will,' said Banford.

And she proceeded to forget about it, except that she was more indignant than ever at the impudence of the beggar. March also was not conscious that she thought of the fox. But whenever she fell into her half-musing, when she was half rapt and half intelligently aware of what passed under her vision, then it was the fox which somehow dominated her unconsciousness, possessed the blank half of her musing. And so it was for weeks, and months. No matter whether she had been climbing the trees for the apples, or beating down the last of the damsons, or whether she had been digging out the ditch from the duck-pond, or clearing out the barn, when she had finished, or when she straightened herself, and pushed the wisps of her hair away again from her forehead, and pursed up her mouth again in an odd, screwed fashion, much too old for her years, there was sure to come over her mind the old spell of the fox, as it came when he was looking at her. It was as if she could smell him at these times. And it always recurred, at unexpected moments, just as she was going to sleep at night, or just as she was pouring the water into the tea-pot to make tea - it was the fox, it came over her like a spell.

So the months passed. She still looked for him unconsciously when she went towards the wood. He had become a settled effect in her spirit, a state permanently established, not continuous, but always recurring. She did not know what she felt or thought: only the state came over her, as when he looked at her.

The months passed, the dark evenings came, heavy, dark November, when March went about in high boots, ankle deep in mud, when the night began to fall at four o'clock, and the day never properly dawned. Both girls dreaded these times. They dreaded the almost continuous darkness that enveloped them on their desolate little farm near the wood. Banford was physically afraid. She was afraid of tramps, afraid lest someone should come prowling around. March was not so much afraid as uncomfortable, and disturbed. She felt discomfort and gloom in all her physique.

Usually the two girls had tea in the sitting-room. March lighted a fire at dusk, and put on the wood she had chopped and sawed during the day. Then the long evening was in front, dark, sodden, black outside, lonely and rather oppressive inside, a little dismal. March was content not to talk, but Banford could not keep still. Merely listening to the wind in the pines outside or the drip of water, was too much for her.

One evening the girls had washed up the tea-cups in the kitchen, and March had put on her house-shoes, and taken up a roll of crochet-work, which she worked at slowly from time to time. So she lapsed into silence. Banford stared at the red fire, which, being of wood, needed constant attention. She was afraid to begin to read too early, because her eyes would not bear any strain. So she sat staring at the fire, listening to the distant sounds, sound of cattle lowing, of a dull, heavy moist wind, of the rattle of the evening train on the little railway not far off. She was almost fascinated by the red glow of the fire.

Suddenly both girls started, and lifted their heads. They heard a footstep - distinctly a footstep. Banford recoiled in fear. March stood listening. Then rapidly she approached the door that led into the kitchen. At the same time they heard the footsteps approach the back door. They waited a second. The back door opened softly. Banford gave a loud cry. A man's voice said softly:

'Hello!'

March recoiled, and took a gun from a corner.

'What do you want?' she cried, in a sharp voice.

Again the soft, softly-vibrating man's voice said:

'Hello! What's wrong!'

'I shall shoot!' cried March. 'What do you want?'

'Why, what's wrong? What's wrong?' came the soft, wondering, rather scared voice: and a young soldier, with his heavy kit on his back, advanced into the dim light.

'Why,' he said, 'who lives here then?'

'We live here,' said March. 'What do you want?'

'Oh!' came the long, melodious, wonder-note from the young soldier. 'Doesn't William Grenfel live here then?'

'No - you know he doesn't.'

'Do I? Do I? I don't, you see. He did LIVE here, because he was my grandfather, and I lived here myself five years ago. What's become of him then?'

The young man - or youth, for he would not be more than twenty - now advanced and stood in the inner doorway. March, already under the influence of his strange, soft, modulated voice, stared at him spellbound. He had a ruddy, roundish face, with fairish hair, rather long, flattened to his forehead with sweat. His eyes were blue, and very bright and sharp. On his cheeks, on the fresh ruddy skin were fine, fair hairs, like a down, but sharper. It gave him a slightly glistening look. Having his heavy sack on his shoulders, he stooped, thrusting his head forward. His hat was loose in one hand. He stared brightly, very keenly from girl to girl, particularly at March, who stood pale, with great dilated eyes, in her belted coat and puttees, her hair knotted in a big crisp knot behind. She still had the gun in her hand. Behind her, Banford, clinging to the sofa-arm, was shrinking away, with half-averted head.

'I thought my grandfather still lived here? I wonder if he's dead.'

'We've been here for three years,' said Banford, who was beginning to recover her wits, seeing something boyish in the round head with its rather long, sweaty hair.

'Three years! You don't say so! And you don't know who was here before you?'

'I know it was an old man, who lived by himself.'

'Ay! Yes, that's him! And what became of him then?'

'He died. I know he died.'

'Ay! He's dead then!'

The youth stared at them without changing colour or expression. If he had any expression, besides a slight baffled look of wonder, it was one of sharp curiosity concerning the two girls; sharp, impersonal curiosity, the curiosity of that round young head.

But to March he was the fox. Whether it was the thrusting forward of his head, or the glisten of fine whitish hairs on the ruddy cheek-bones, or the bright, keen eyes, that can never be said: but the boy was to her the fox, and she could not see him otherwise.

'How is it you didn't know if your grandfather was alive or dead?' asked Banford, recovering her natural sharpness.

'Ay, that's it,' replied the softly-breathing youth. 'You see, I joined up in Canada, and I hadn't heard for three or four years. I ran away to Canada.'

'And now have you just come from France?'

'Well - from Salonika really.'

There was a pause, nobody knowing quite what to say.

'So you've nowhere to go now?' said Banford rather lamely.

'Oh, I know some people in the village. Anyhow, I can go to the "Swan".'

'You came on the train, I suppose. Would you like to sit down a bit?'

'Well - I don't mind.'

He gave an odd little groan as he swung off his kit. Banford looked at March.

'Put the gun down,' she said. 'We'll make a cup of tea.'

'Ay,' said the youth. 'We've seen enough of rifles.'

He sat down rather tired on the sofa, leaning forward.

March recovered her presence of mind, and went into the kitchen. There she heard the soft young voice musing:

'Well, to think I should come back and find it like this!' He did not seem sad, not at all - only rather interestedly surprised.

'And what a difference in the place, eh?' he continued, looking round the room.

'You see a difference, do you?' said Banford.

'Yes - don't I!'

His eyes were unnaturally clear and bright, though it was the brightness of abundant health.

March was busy in the kitchen preparing another meal. It was about seven o'clock. All the time, while she was active, she was attending to the youth in the sitting-room, not so much listening to what he said as

75

feeling the soft run of his voice. She primmed up her mouth tighter and tighter, puckering it as if it were sewed, in her effort to keep her will uppermost. Yet her large eyes dilated and glowed in spite of her; she lost herself. Rapidly and carelessly she prepared the meal, cutting large chunks of bread and margarine - for there was no butter. She racked her brain to think of something else to put on the tray - she had only bread, margarine, and jam, and the larder was bare. Unable to conjure anything up, she went into the sitting-room with her tray.

She did not want to be noticed. Above all, she did not want him to look at her. But when she came in, and was busy setting the table just behind him, he pulled himself up from his sprawling, and turned and looked over his shoulder. She became pale and wan.

The youth watched her as she bent over the table, looked at her slim, well-shapen legs, at the belted coat dropping around her thighs, at the knot of dark hair, and his curiosity, vivid and widely alert, was again arrested by her.

The lamp was shaded with a dark-green shade, so that the light was thrown downwards and the upper half of the room was dim. His face moved bright under the light, but March loomed shadowy in the distance.

She turned round, but kept her eyes sideways, dropping and lifting her dark lashes. Her mouth unpuckered as she said to Banford:

'Will you pour out?'

Then she went into the kitchen again.

'Have your tea where you are, will you?' said Banford to the youth - 'unless you'd rather come to the table.'

'Well,' said he, 'I'm nice and comfortable here, aren't I? I will have it here, if you don't mind.'

'There's nothing but bread and jam,' she said. And she put his plate on a stool by him. She was very happy now, waiting on him. For she loved company. And now she was no more afraid of him than if he were her own younger brother. He was such a boy.

'Nellie,' she called. 'I've poured you a cup out.'

March appeared in the doorway, took her cup, and sat down in a corner, as far from the light as possible. She was very sensitive in her knees. Having no skirts to cover them, and being forced to sit with them boldly exposed, she suffered. She shrank and shrank, trying not to be seen. And the youth sprawling low on the couch, glanced up at her, with long, steady, penetrating looks, till she was almost ready to disappear. Yet she held her cup balanced, she drank her tea, screwed up her mouth and held her head averted. Her desire to be invisible was so strong that it quite baffled the youth. He felt he could not see her distinctly. She seemed like a shadow within the shadow. And ever his eyes came back to her, searching, unremitting, with unconscious fixed attention.

Meanwhile he was talking softly and smoothly to Banford, who loved nothing so much as gossip, and who was full of perky interest, like a bird. Also he ate largely and quickly and voraciously, so that March had to cut more chunks of bread and margarine, for the roughness of which Banford apologized.

'Oh, well,' said March, suddenly speaking, 'if there's no butter to put on it, it's no good trying to make dainty pieces.'

Again the youth watched her, and he laughed, with a sudden, quick laugh, showing his teeth and wrinkling his nose.

'It isn't, is it,' he answered in his soft, near voice.

It appeared he was Cornish by birth and upbringing. When he was twelve years old he had come to Bailey Farm with his grandfather, with whom he had never agreed very well. So he had run away to Canada, and worked far away in the West. Now he was here - and that was the end of it.

He was very curious about the girls, to find out exactly what they were doing. His questions were those of a farm youth; acute, practical, a little mocking. He was very much amused by their attitude to their losses: for they were amusing on the score of heifers and fowls.

'Oh, well,' broke in March, 'we don't believe in living for nothing but work.'

'Don't you?' he answered. And again the quick young laugh came over his face. He kept his eyes steadily on the obscure woman in the corner.

'But what will you do when you've used up all your capital?' he said.

'Oh, I don't know,' answered March laconically. 'Hire ourselves out for land-workers, I suppose.'

'Yes, but there won't be any demand for women land-workers now the war's over,' said the youth.

'Oh, we'll see. We shall hold on a bit longer yet,' said March, with a plangent, half-sad, half-ironical indifference.

'There wants a man about the place,' said the youth softly.

Banford burst out laughing.

'Take care what you say,' she interrupted. 'We consider ourselves quite efficient.'

'Oh,' came March's slow plangent voice, 'it isn't a case of efficiency, I'm afraid. If you're going to do farming you must be at it from morning till night, and you might as well be a beast yourself.'

'Yes, that's it,' said the youth. 'You aren't willing to put yourselves into it.'

'We aren't,' said March, 'and we know it.'

'We want some of our time for ourselves,' said Banford.

The youth threw himself back on the sofa, his face tight with laughter, and laughed silently but thoroughly. The calm scorn of the girls tickled him tremendously.

'Yes,' he said, 'but why did you begin then?'

'Oh,' said March, 'we had a better opinion of the nature of fowls then than we have now.'

'Of Nature altogether, I'm afraid,' said Banford. 'Don't talk to me about Nature.'

Again the face of the youth tightened with delighted laughter.

'You haven't a very high opinion of fowls and cattle, have you?' he said.

'Oh no - quite a low one,' said March.

He laughed out.

'Neither fowls nor heifers,' said Banford, 'nor goats nor the weather.'

The youth broke into a sharp yap of laughter, delighted. The girls began to laugh too, March turning aside her face and wrinkling her mouth in amusement.

'Oh, well,' said Banford, 'we don't mind, do we, Nellie?'

'No,' said March, 'we don't mind.'

The youth was very pleased. He had eaten and drunk his fill. Banford began to question him. His name was Henry Grenfel - no, he was not called Harry, always Henry. He continued to answer with courteous simplicity, grave and charming. March, who was not included, cast long, slow glances at him from her recess, as he sat there on the sofa, his hands clasping his knees, his face under the lamp bright and alert, turned to Banford. She became almost peaceful at last. He was identified with the fox - and he was here in full presence. She need not go after him any more. There in the shadow of her corner she gave herself up to a warm, relaxed peace, almost like sleep, accepting the spell that was on her. But she wished to remain hidden. She was only fully at peace whilst he forgot her, talking to Banford. Hidden in the shadow of the corner, she need not any more be divided in herself, trying to keep up two planes of consciousness. She could at last lapse into the odour of the fox.

For the youth, sitting before the fire in his uniform, sent a faint but distinct odour into the room, indefinable, but something like a wild creature. March no longer tried to reserve herself from it. She was still and soft in her corner like a passive creature in its cave.

At last the talk dwindled. The youth relaxed his clasp of his knees, pulled himself together a little, and looked round. Again he became aware of the silent, half-invisible woman in the corner.

'Well,' he said unwillingly, 'I suppose I'd better be going, or they'll be in bed at the "Swan ".'

'I'm afraid they're in bed, anyhow,' said Banford. 'They've all got this influenza.'

'Have they!' he exclaimed. And he pondered. 'Well,' he continued, 'I shall find a place somewhere.'

'I'd say you could stay here, only -' Banford began.

He turned and watched her, holding his head forward.

'What?' he asked.

'Oh, well,' she said, 'propriety, I suppose.' She was rather confused.

'It wouldn't be improper, would it?' he said, gently surprised.

'Not as far as we're concerned,' said Banford.

'And not as far as I'M concerned,' he said, with grave naivete. 'After all, it's my own home, in a way.'

Banford smiled at this.

'It's what the village will have to say,' she said.

There was a moment's blank pause.

'What do you say, Nellie?' asked Banford.

'I don't mind,' said March, in her distinct tone. 'The village doesn't matter to me, anyhow.'

'No,' said the youth, quick and soft. 'Why should it? I mean, what should they say?'

'Oh, well,' came March's plangent, laconic voice, 'they'll easily find something to say. But it makes no difference what they say. We can look after ourselves.'

'Of course you can,' said the youth.

'Well then, stop if you like,' said Banford. 'The spare room is quite ready.'

His face shone with pleasure.

'If you're quite sure it isn't troubling you too much,' he said, with that soft courtesy which distinguished him.

'Oh, it's no trouble,' they both said.

He looked, smiling with delight, from one to another.

'It's awfully nice not to have to turn out again, isn't it?' he said gratefully.

'I suppose it is,' said Banford.

March disappeared to attend the room. Banford was as pleased and thoughtful as if she had her own young brother home from France. It gave her just the same kind of gratification to attend on him, to get out the bath for him, and everything. Her natural warmth and kindliness had now an outlet. And the youth luxuriated in her sisterly attention. But it puzzled him slightly to know that March was silently working for him too. She was so curiously silent and obliterated. It seemed to him he had not really seen her. He felt he should not know her if he met her in the road.

That night March dreamed vividly. She dreamed she heard a singing outside which she could not understand, a singing that roamed round the house, in the fields, and in the darkness. It moved her so that she felt she must weep. She went out, and suddenly she knew it was the fox singing. He was very yellow and bright, like corn. She went nearer to him, but he ran away and ceased singing. He seemed near, and she wanted to touch him. She stretched out her hand, but suddenly he bit her wrist, and at the same instant, as she drew back, the fox, turning round to bound away, whisked his brush across her face, and it seemed his brush was on fire, for it seared and burned her mouth with a great pain. She awoke with the pain of it, and lay trembling as if she were really seared.

In the morning, however, she only remembered it as a distant memory. She arose and was busy preparing the house and attending to the fowls. Banford flew into the village on her bicycle to try and buy food. She was a hospitable soul. But alas, in the year 1918 there was not much food to buy. The youth came downstairs in his shirt-sleeves. He was young and fresh, but he walked with his head thrust forward, so that his shoulders seemed raised and rounded, as if he had a slight curvature of the spine. It must have been only a manner of bearing himself, for he was young and vigorous. He washed himself and went outside, whilst the women were preparing breakfast.

He saw everything, and examined everything. His curiosity was quick and insatiable. He compared the state of things with that which he remembered before, and cast over in his mind the effect of the changes. He watched the fowls and the ducks, to see their condition; he noticed the flight of wood-pigeons overhead: they were very numerous; he saw the few apples high up, which March had not been able to reach; he remarked that they had borrowed a draw-pump, presumably to empty the big soft-water cistern which was on the north side of the house.

'It's a funny, dilapidated old place,' he said to the girls, as he sat at breakfast.

His eyes were wise and childish, with thinking about things. He did not say much, but ate largely. March kept her face averted. She, too, in the early morning could not be aware of him, though something about the glint of his khaki reminded her of the brilliance of her dream-fox.

During the day the girls went about their business. In the morning he attended to the guns, shot a rabbit and a wild duck that was flying high towards the wood. That was a great addition to the empty larder. The girls felt that already he had earned his keep. He said nothing about leaving, however. In the afternoon he went to the village. He came back at tea-time. He had the same alert, forward-reaching look on his roundish face. He hung his hat on a peg with a little swinging gesture. He was thinking about something.

'Well,' he said to the girls, as he sat at table. 'What am I going to do?'

'How do you mean - what are you going to do?' said Banford.

'Where am I going to find a place in the village to stay?' he said.

'I don't know,' said Banford. 'Where do you think of staying?'

'Well' - he hesitated - 'at the "Swan" they've got this flu, and at the "Plough and Harrow" they've got the soldiers who are collecting the hay for the army: besides, in the private houses, there's ten men and a corporal altogether billeted in the village, they tell me. I'm not sure where I could get a bed.'

He left the matter to them. He was rather calm about it. March sat with her elbows on the table, her two hands supporting her chin, looking at him unconsciously. Suddenly he lifted his clouded blue eyes, and unthinking looked straight into March's eyes. He was startled as well as she. He, too, recoiled a little. March felt the same sly, taunting, knowing spark leap out of his eyes, as he turned his head aside, and fall into her soul, as it had fallen from the dark eyes of the fox. She pursed her mouth as if in pain, as if asleep too.

'Well, I don't know,' Banford was saying. She seemed reluctant, as if she were afraid of being imposed upon. She looked at March. But, with her weak, troubled sight, she only saw the usual semi-abstraction on her friend's face. 'Why don't you speak, Nellie?' she said.

But March was wide-eyed and silent, and the youth, as if fascinated, was watching her without moving his eyes.

'Go on - answer something,' said Banford. And March turned her head slightly aside, as if coming to consciousness, or trying to come to consciousness.

'What do you expect me to say?' she asked automatically.

'Say what you think,' said Banford.

'It's all the same to me,' said March.

And again there was silence. A pointed light seemed to be on the boy's eyes, penetrating like a needle.

'So it is to me,' said Banford. 'You can stop on here if you like.'

A smile like a cunning little flame came over his face, suddenly and involuntarily. He dropped his head quickly to hide it, and remained with his head dropped, his face hidden.

'You can stop on here if you like. You can please yourself, Henry,' Banford concluded.

Still he did not reply, but remained with his head dropped. Then he lifted his face. It was bright with a curious light, as if exultant, and his eyes were strangely clear as he watched March. She turned her face aside, her mouth suffering as if wounded, and her consciousness dim.

Banford became a little puzzled. She watched the steady, pellucid gaze of the youth's eyes as he looked at March, with the invisible smile gleaming on his face. She did not know how he was smiling, for no feature moved. It seemed only in the gleam, almost the glitter of the fine hairs on his cheeks. Then he looked with quite a changed look at Banford.

'I'm sure,' he said in his soft, courteous voice, 'you're awfully good. You're too good. You don't want to be bothered with me, I'm sure.'

'Cut a bit of bread, Nellie,' said Banford uneasily, adding: 'It's no bother, if you like to stay. It's like having my own brother here for a few days. He's a boy like you are.'

'That's awfully kind of you,' the lad repeated. 'I should like to stay ever so much, if you're sure I'm not a trouble to you.'

'No, of course you're no trouble. I tell you, it's a pleasure to have somebody in the house beside ourselves,' said warmhearted Banford.

'But Miss March?' he said in his soft voice, looking at her.

'Oh, it's quite all right as far as I'm concerned,' said March vaguely.

His face beamed, and he almost rubbed his hands with pleasure.

'Well then,' he said, 'I should love it, if you'd let me pay my board and help with the work.'

'You've no need to talk about board,' said Banford.

One or two days went by, and the youth stayed on at the farm. Banford was quite charmed by him. He was so soft and courteous in speech, not wanting to say much himself, preferring to hear what she had to say, and to laugh in his quick, half-mocking way. He helped readily with the work - but not too much. He loved to be out alone with the gun in his hands, to watch, to see. For his sharp-eyed, impersonal curiosity was insatiable, and he was most free when he was quite alone, half-hidden, watching.

Particularly he watched March. She was a strange character to him. Her figure, like a graceful young man's, piqued him. Her dark eyes made something rise in his soul, with a curious elate excitement, when he looked into them, an excitement he was afraid to let be seen, it was so keen and secret. And then her odd, shrewd speech made him laugh outright. He felt he must go further, he was inevitably impelled. But he put away the thought of her and went off towards the wood's edge with the gun.

The dusk was falling as he came home, and with the dusk, a fine, late November rain. He saw the fire-light leaping in the window of the sitting-room, a leaping light in the little cluster of the dark buildings. And he thought to himself it would be a good thing to have this place for his own. And then the thought entered him shrewdly: Why not marry March? He stood still in the middle of the field for some moments, the dead rabbit hanging still in his hand, arrested by this thought. His mind waited in amazement - it seemed to calculate - and then he smiled curiously to himself in acquiescence. Why not? Why not indeed? It was a good idea. What if it was rather ridiculous? What did it matter? What if she was older than he? It didn't matter. When he thought of her dark, startled, vulnerable eyes he smiled subtly to himself. He was older than she, really. He was master of her.

He scarcely admitted his intention even to himself. He kept it as a secret even from himself. It was all too uncertain as yet. He would have to see how things went. Yes, he would have to see how things went. If he wasn't careful, she would just simply mock at the idea. He knew, sly and subtle as he was, that if he went to her plainly and said: 'Miss March, I love you and want you to marry me,' her inevitable answer would be: 'Get out. I don't want any of that tomfoolery.' This was her attitude to men and their 'tomfoolery'. If he was not careful, she would turn round on him with her savage, sardonic ridicule, and dismiss him from the farm and from her own mind for ever. He would have to go gently. He would have to catch her as you catch a deer or a woodcock when you go out shooting. It's no good walking out into the forest and saying to the deer: 'Please fall to my gun.' No, it is a slow, subtle battle. When you really go out to get a deer, you gather yourself together, you coil yourself inside yourself, and you advance secretly, before dawn, into the mountains. It is not so much what you do, when you go out hunting, as how you feel. You have to be subtle and cunning and absolutely fatally ready. It becomes like a fate. Your own fate overtakes and determines the fate of the deer you are hunting. First of all, even before you come in sight of your quarry, there is a strange battle, like mesmerism. Your own soul, as a hunter, has gone out to fasten on the soul of the deer, even before you see any deer. And the soul of the deer fights to escape. Even before the deer has any wind of you, it is so. It is a subtle, profound battle of wills which takes place in the invisible. And it is a battle never finished till your bullet goes home. When you are REALLY worked up to the true pitch, and you come at last into range, you don't then aim as you do when you are firing at a bottle. It is your own WILL which carries the bullet into the heart of your quarry. The bullet's flight home is a sheer projection of your own fate into the fate of the deer. It happens like a supreme wish, a supreme act of volition, not as a dodge of cleverness.

He was a huntsman in spirit, not a farmer, and not a soldier stuck in a regiment. And it was as a young hunter that he wanted to bring down March as his quarry, to make her his wife. So he gathered himself subtly together, seemed to withdraw into a kind of invisibility. He was not quite sure how he would go on. And March was suspicious as a hare. So he remained in appearance just the nice, odd stranger-youth, staying for a fortnight on the place.

He had been sawing logs for the fire in the afternoon. Darkness came very early. It was still a cold, raw mist. It was getting almost too dark to see. A pile of short sawed logs lay beside the trestle. March came to carry them indoors, or into the shed, as he was busy sawing the last log. He was working in his shirt-sleeves, and did not notice her approach; she came unwillingly, as if shy. He saw her stooping to the bright-ended logs, and he stopped sawing. A fire like lightning flew down his legs in the nerves.

'March?' he said in his quiet, young voice.

She looked up from the logs she was piling.

'Yes!' she said.

He looked down on her in the dusk. He could see her not too distinctly.

'I wanted to ask you something,' he said.

'Did you? What was it?' she said. Already the fright was in her voice. But she was too much mistress of herself.

'Why' - his voice seemed to draw out soft and subtle, it penetrated her nerves - 'why, what do you think it is?'

She stood up, placed her hands on her hips, and stood looking at him transfixed, without answering. Again he burned with a sudden power.

'Well,' he said, and his voice was so soft it seemed rather like a subtle touch, like the merest touch of a cat's paw, a feeling rather than a sound.' Well - I wanted to ask you to marry me.'

March felt rather than heard him. She was trying in vain to turn aside her face. A great relaxation seemed to have come over her. She stood silent, her head slightly on one side. He seemed to be bending towards her, invisibly smiling. It seemed to her fine sparks came out of him.

Then very suddenly she said:

'Don't try any of your tomfoolery on me.'

A quiver went over his nerves. He had missed. He waited a moment to collect himself again. Then he said, putting all the strange softness into his voice, as if he were imperceptibly stroking her:

'Why, it's not tomfoolery. It's not tomfoolery. I mean it. I mean it. What makes you disbelieve me?'

He sounded hurt. And his voice had such a curious power over her; making her feel loose and relaxed. She struggled somewhere for her own power. She felt for a moment that she was lost - lost - lost. The word seemed to rock in her as if she were dying. Suddenly again she spoke.

'You don't know what you are talking about,' she said, in a brief and transient stroke of scorn. 'What nonsense! I'm old enough to be your mother.'

'Yes, I do know what I'm talking about. Yes, I do,' he persisted softly, as if he were producing his voice in her blood. 'I know quite well what I'm talking about. You're not old enough to be my mother. That isn't true. And what does it matter even if it was. You can marry me whatever age we are. What is age to me? And what is age to you! Age is nothing.'

A swoon went over her as he concluded. He spoke rapidly - in the rapid Cornish fashion - and his voice seemed to sound in her somewhere where she was helpless against it. 'Age is nothing!' The soft, heavy insistence of it made her sway dimly out there in the darkness. She could not answer.

A great exultance leaped like fire over his limbs. He felt he had won.

'I want to marry you, you see. Why shouldn't I?' he proceeded, soft and rapid. He waited for her to answer. In the dusk he saw her almost phosphorescent. Her eyelids were dropped, her face half-averted and unconscious. She seemed to be in his power. But he waited, watchful. He dared not yet touch her.

86

'Say then,' he said, 'say then you'll marry me. Say - say!' He was softly insistent.

'What?' she asked, faint, from a distance, like one in pain. His voice was now unthinkably near and soft. He drew very near to her.

'Say yes.'

'Oh, I can't,' she wailed helplessly, half-articulate, as if semiconscious, and as if in pain, like one who dies. 'How can I?'

'You can,' he said softly, laying his hand gently on her shoulder as she stood with her head averted and dropped, dazed. 'You can. Yes, you can. What makes you say you can't? You can. You can.' And with awful softness he bent forward and just touched her neck with his mouth and his chin.

'Don't!' she cried, with a faint mad cry like hysteria, starting away and facing round on him. 'What do you mean?' But she had no breath to speak with. It was as if she was killed.

'I mean what I say,' he persisted softly and cruelly. 'I want you to marry me. I want you to marry me. You know that, now, don't you? You know that, now? Don't you? Don't you?'

'What?' she said.

'Know,' he replied.

'Yes,' she said. 'I know you say so.'

'And you know I mean it, don't you?'

'I know you say so.'

'You believe me?' he said.

She was silent for some time. Then she pursed her lips.

'I don't know what I believe,' she said.

'Are you out there?' came Banford's voice, calling from the house.

'Yes, we're bringing in the logs,' he answered.

'I thought you'd gone lost,' said Banford disconsolately. 'Hurry up, do, and come and let's have tea. The kettle's boiling.'

He stooped at once to take an armful of little logs and carry them into the kitchen, where they were piled in a corner. March also helped, filling her arms and carrying the logs on her breast as if they were some heavy child. The night had fallen cold.

When the logs were all in, the two cleaned their boots noisily on the scraper outside, then rubbed them on the mat. March shut the door and took off her old felt hat - her farm-girl hat. Her thick, crisp, black hair was loose, her face was pale and strained. She pushed back her hair vaguely and washed her hands. Banford came hurrying into the dimly-lighted kitchen, to take from the oven the scones she was keeping hot.

'Whatever have you been doing all this time?' she asked fretfully. 'I thought you were never coming in. And it's ages since you stopped sawing. What were you doing out there?'

'Well,' said Henry, 'we had to stop that hole in the barn to keeps the rats out.'

'Why, I could see you standing there in the shed. I could see your shirt-sleeves,' challenged Banford.

'Yes, I was just putting the saw away.'

They went in to tea. March was quite mute. Her face was pale and strained and vague. The youth, who always had the same ruddy, self-contained look on his face, as though he were keeping himself to himself, had come to tea in his shirt-sleeves as if he were at home. He bent over his plate as he ate his food.

'Aren't you cold?' said Banford spitefully. 'In your shirtsleeves.'

He looked up at her, with his chin near his plate, and his eyes very clear, pellucid, and unwavering as he watched her.

'No, I'm not cold,' he said with his usual soft courtesy. 'It's much warmer in here than it is outside, you see.'

'I hope it is,' said Banford, feeling nettled by him. He had a strange, suave assurance and a wide-eyed bright look that got on her nerves this evening.

'But perhaps,' he said softly and courteously, 'you don't like me coming to tea without my coat. I forgot that.'

'Oh, I don't mind,' said Banford: although she DID.

'I'll go and get it, shall I?' he said.

March's dark eyes turned slowly down to him.

'No, don't you bother,' she said in her queer, twanging tone. 'If you feel all right as you are, stop as you are.' She spoke with a crude authority.

'Yes,' said he, 'I FEEL all right, if I'm not rude.'

'It's usually considered rude,' said Banford. 'But we don't mind.'

'Go along, "considered rude",' ejaculated March. 'Who considers it rude?'

'Why, you do, Nellie, in anybody else,' said Banford, bridling a little behind her spectacles, and feeling her food stick in her throat.

But March had again gone vague and unheeding, chewing her food as if she did not know she was eating at all. And the youth looked from one to another, with bright, watching eyes.

Banford was offended. For all his suave courtesy and soft voice, the youth seemed to her impudent. She did not like to look at him. She did not like to meet his clear, watchful eyes, she did not like to see the strange glow in his face, his cheeks with their delicate fine hair, and his ruddy skin that was quite dull and yet which seemed to burn with a curious heat of life. It made her feel a little ill to look at him: the quality of his physical presence was too penetrating, too hot.

After tea the evening was very quiet. The youth rarely went into the village. As a rule, he read: he was a great reader, in his own hours. That is, when he did begin, he read absorbedly. But he was not very eager to begin. Often he walked about the fields and along the hedges alone in the dark at night, prowling with a queer instinct for the night, and listening to the wild sounds.

Tonight, however, he took a Captain Mayne Reid book from Banford's shelf and sat down with knees wide apart and immersed himself in his story. His brownish fair hair was long, and lay on his head like a thick cap, combed sideways. He was still in his shirt-sleeves, and bending forward under the lamplight, with his knees stuck wide apart and the book in his hand and his whole figure absorbed in the rather strenuous business of reading, he gave Banford's sitting-room the look of a lumber-camp. She resented this. For on her sitting-room floor she had a red Turkey rug and dark stain round, the fire-place had fashionable green tiles, the piano stood open with the latest dance music: she played quite well: and on the walls were March's hand-painted swans and water-lilies. Moreover, with the logs nicely, tremulously burning in the grate, the thick curtains drawn, the doors all shut, and the pine trees hissing and shuddering in the wind outside, it was cosy, it was refined and nice. She resented the big, raw, long-legged youth sticking his khaki knees out and sitting there with his soldier's shirt-cuffs buttoned on his thick red wrists. From time to time he turned a page, and from time to time he gave a sharp look at the fire, settling the logs. Then he immersed himself again in the intense and isolated business of reading.

March, on the far side of the table, was spasmodically crocheting.

Her mouth was pursed in an odd way, as when she had dreamed the fox's brush burned it, her beautiful, crisp black hair strayed in wisps. But her whole figure was absorbed in its bearing, as if she herself was miles away. In a sort of semi-dream she seemed to be hearing the fox singing round the house in the wind, singing wildly and sweetly and like a madness. With red but well-shaped hands she slowly crocheted the white cotton, very slowly, awkwardly.

Banford was also trying to read, sitting in her low chair. But between those two she felt fidgety. She kept moving and looking round and listening to the wind, and glancing secretly from one to the other of her companions. March, seated on a straight chair, with her knees in their close breeches crossed, and slowly, laboriously crocheting, was also a trial.

'Oh dear!' said Banford, 'My eyes are bad tonight.' And she pressed her fingers on her eyes.

The youth looked up at her with his clear, bright look, but did not speak.

'Are they, Jill?' said March absently.

Then the youth began to read again, and Banford perforce returned to her book. But she could not keep still. After a while she looked up at March, and a queer, almost malignant little smile was on her thin face.

'A penny for them, Nell,' she said suddenly.

March looked round with big, startled black eyes, and went pale as if with terror. She had been listening to the fox singing so tenderly, so tenderly, as he wandered round the house.

'What?' she said vaguely.

'A penny for them,' said Banford sarcastically. 'Or twopence, if they're as deep as all that.'

The youth was watching with bright, clear eyes from beneath the lamp.

'Why,' came March's vague voice, 'what do you want to waste your money for?'

'I thought it would be well spent,' said Banford.

'I wasn't thinking of anything except the way the wind was blowing,' said March.

'Oh dear,' replied Banford, 'I could have had as original thought as that myself. I'm afraid I HAVE wasted my money this time.'

'Well, you needn't pay,' said March.

The youth suddenly laughed. Both women looked at him: March rather surprised-looking, as if she had hardly known he was there.

'Why, do you ever pay up on these occasions?' he asked.

'Oh yes,' said Banford. 'We always do. I've sometimes had to pass a shilling a week to Nellie, in the winter-time. It costs much less in summer.'

'What, paying for each other's thoughts?' he laughed.

'Yes, when we've absolutely come to the end of everything else.'

He laughed quickly, wrinkling his nose sharply like a puppy and laughing with quick pleasure, his eyes shining.

'It's the first time I ever heard of that,' he said.

'I guess you'd hear of it often enough if you stayed a winter on Bailey Farm,' said Banford lamentably.

'Do you get so tired, then?' he asked.

'So bored,' said Banford.

'Oh!' he said gravely. 'But why should you be bored?'

'Who wouldn't be bored?' said Banford.

'I'm sorry to hear that,' he said gravely.

'You must be, if you were hoping to have a lively time here,' said Banford.

He looked at her long and gravely.

'Well,' he said, with his odd, young seriousness, 'it's quite lively enough for me.'

'I'm glad to hear it,' said Banford.

And she returned to her book. In her thin, frail hair were already many threads of grey, though she was not yet thirty. The boy did not look down, but turned his eyes to March, who was sitting with pursed mouth laboriously crocheting, her eyes wide and absent. She had a warm, pale, fine skin and a delicate nose. Her pursed mouth looked shrewish. But the shrewish look was contradicted by the curious lifted arch of her dark brows, and the wideness of her eyes; a look of startled wonder and vagueness. She was listening again for the fox, who seemed to have wandered farther off into the night.

From under the edge of the lamp-light the boy sat with his face looking up, watching her silently, his eyes round and very clear and intent. Banford, biting her fingers irritably, was glancing at him under her hair. He sat there perfectly still, his ruddy face tilted up from the low level under the light, on the edge of the dimness, and watching with perfect abstract intentness. March suddenly lifted her great, dark eyes from her crocheting and saw him. She started, giving a little exclamation.

'There he is!' she cried involuntarily, as if terribly startled.

Banford looked round in amazement, sitting up straight.

'Whatever has got you, Nellie?' she cried.

But March, her face flushed a delicate rose colour, was looking away to the door.

'Nothing! Nothing!' she said crossly. 'Can't one speak?'

'Yes, if you speak sensibly,' said Banford. 'What ever did you mean?'

'I don't know what I meant,' cried March testily

Oh, Nellie, I hope you aren't going jumpy and nervy. I feel I can't stand another THING! Whoever did you mean? Did you mean Henry?' cried poor, frightened Banford.

'Yes. I suppose so,' said March laconically. She would never confess to the fox.

'Oh dear, my nerves are all gone for tonight,' wailed Banford.

At nine o'clock March brought in a tray with bread and cheese and tea - Henry had confessed that he liked a cup of tea. Banford drank a glass of milk and ate a little bread. And soon she said:

'I'm going to bed, Nellie, I'm all nerves tonight. Are you coming?'

'Yes, I'm coming the minute I've taken the tray away,' said March.

'Don't be long then,' said Banford fretfully. 'Good-night, Henry. You'll see the fire is safe, if you come up last, won't you?'

'Yes, Miss Banford, I'll see it's safe,' he replied in his reassuring way.

March was lighting the candle to go to the kitchen. Banford took her candle and went upstairs. When March came back to the fire, she said to him:

'I suppose we can trust you to put out the fire and everything?' She stood there with her hand on her hip, and one knee loose, her head averted shyly, as if she could not look at him. He had his face lifted, watching her.

'Come and sit down a minute,' he said softly.

'No, I'll be going. Jill will be waiting, and she'll get upset, if I don't come.'

'What made you jump like that this evening?' he asked.

'When did I jump?' she retorted, looking at him.

'Why, just now you did,' he said. 'When you cried out.'

'Oh!' she said. 'Then! - Why, I thought you were the fox!' And her face screwed into a queer smile, half-ironic.

'The fox! Why the fox?' he asked softly.

'Why, one evening last summer when I was out with the gun I saw the fox in the grass nearly at my feet, looking straight up at me. I don't know - I suppose he made an impression on me.' She turned aside her head again and let one foot stray loose, self-consciously.

'And did you shoot him?' asked the boy.

'No, he gave me such a start, staring straight at me as he did, and then stopping to look back at me over his shoulder with a laugh on his face.'

'A laugh on his face!' repeated Henry, also laughing. 'He frightened you, did he?'

'No, he didn't frighten me. He made an impression on me, that's all.'

'And you thought I was the fox, did you?' he laughed, with the same queer, quick little laugh, like a puppy wrinkling his nose.

'Yes, I did, for the moment,' she said. 'Perhaps he'd been in my mind without my knowing.'

'Perhaps you think I've come to steal your chickens or something,' he said, with the same young laugh.

But she only looked at him with a wide, dark, vacant eye.

'It's the first time,' he said, 'that I've ever been taken for a fox. Won't you sit down for a minute?' His voice was very soft and cajoling.

'No,' she said. 'Jill will be waiting.' But still she did not go, but stood with one foot loose and her face turned aside, just outside the circle of light.

'But won't you answer my question?' he said, lowering his voice still more.

'I don't know what question you mean.'

'Yes, you do. Of course you do. I mean the question of you marrying me.'

'No, I shan't answer that question,' she said flatly.

'Won't you?' The queer, young laugh came on his nose again. 'Is it because I'm like the fox? Is that why?' And still he laughed.

She turned and looked at him with a long, slow look.

'I wouldn't let that put you against me,' he said. 'Let me turn the lamp low, and come and sit down a minute.'

He put his red hand under the glow of the lamp and suddenly made the light very dim. March stood there in the dimness quite shadowy, but unmoving. He rose silently to his feet, on his long legs. And now his voice was extraordinarily soft and suggestive, hardly audible.

'You'll stay a moment,' he said. 'Just a moment.' And he put his hand on her shoulder. She turned her face from him. 'I'm sure you don't really think I'm like the fox,' he said, with the same softness and with a suggestion of laughter in his tone, a subtle mockery. 'Do you now?' And he drew her gently towards him and kissed her neck, softly. She winced and trembled and hung away. But his strong, young arm held her, and he kissed her softly again, still on the neck, for her face was averted.

'Won't you answer my question? Won't you now?' came his soft, lingering voice. He was trying to draw her near to kiss her face. And he kissed her cheek softly, near the ear.

At that moment Banford's voice was heard calling fretfully, crossly from upstairs.

'There's Jill!' cried March, starting and drawing erect.

And as she did so, quick as lightning he kissed her on the mouth, with a quick, brushing kiss. It seemed to burn through her every fibre. She gave a queer little cry.

'You will, won't you? You will?' he insisted softly.

'Nellie! NELLIE! What ever are you so long for?' came Banford's faint cry from the outer darkness.

But he held her fast, and was murmuring with that intolerable softness and insistency:

'You will, won't you? Say yes! Say yes!'

March, who felt as if the fire had gone through her and scathed her, and as if she could do no more, murmured:

'Yes! Yes! Anything you like! Anything you like! Only let me go! Only let me go! Jill's calling.'

'You know you've promised,' he said insidiously.

'Yes! Yes! I do!' Her voice suddenly rose into a shrill cry. 'All right, Jill, I'm coming.'

Startled, he let her go, and she went straight upstairs.

94

In the morning at breakfast, after he had looked round the place and attended to the stock and thought to himself that one could live easily enough here, he said to Banford:

'Do you know what, Miss Banford?'

'Well, what?' said the good-natured, nervy Banford.

He looked at March, who was spreading jam on her bread.

'Shall I tell?' he said to her.

She looked up at him, and a deep pink colour flushed over her face.

'Yes, if you mean Jill,' she said. 'I hope you won't go talking all over the village, that's all.' And she swallowed her dry bread with difficulty.

'Whatever's coming?' said Banford, looking up with wide, tired, slightly reddened eyes. She was a thin, frail little thing, and her hair, which was delicate and thin, was bobbed, so it hung softly by her worn face in its faded brown and grey.

'Why, what do you think?' he said, smiling like one who has a secret.

'How do I know!' said Banford.

'Can't you guess?' he said, making bright eyes and smiling, pleased with himself.

'I'm sure I can't. What's more, I'm not going to try.'

'Nellie and I are going to be married.'

Banford put down her knife out of her thin, delicate fingers, as if she would never take it up to eat any more. She stared with blank, reddened eyes.

'You what?' she exclaimed.

'We're going to get married. Aren't we, Nellie?' and he turned to March.

'You say so, anyway,' said March laconically. But again she flushed with an agonized flush. She, too, could swallow no more.

Banford looked at her like a bird that has been shot: a poor, little sick bird. She gazed at her with all her wounded soul in her face, at the deep-flushed March.

'Never!' she exclaimed, helpless.

'It's quite right,' said the bright and gloating youth.

Banford turned aside her face, as if the sight of the food on the table made her sick. She sat like this for some moments, as if she were sick. Then, with one hand on the edge of the table, she rose to her feet.

'I'll NEVER believe it, Nellie,' she cried. 'It's absolutely impossible!'

Her plaintive, fretful voice had a thread of hot anger and despair.

'Why? Why shouldn't you believe it?' asked the youth, with all his soft, velvety impertinence in his voice.

Banford looked at him from her wide, vague eyes, as if he were some creature in a museum.

'Oh,' she said languidly, 'because she can never be such a fool. She can't lose her self-respect to such an extent.' Her voice was cold and plaintive, drifting.

'In what way will she lose her self-respect?' asked the boy.

Banford looked at him with vague fixity from behind her spectacles.

'If she hasn't lost it already,' she said.

He became very red, vermilion, under the slow, vague stare from behind the spectacles.

'I don't see it at all,' he said.

'Probably you don't. I shouldn't expect you would,' said Banford, with that straying, mild tone of remoteness which made her words even more insulting.

He sat stiff in his chair, staring with hot, blue eyes from his scarlet face. An ugly look had come on his brow.

'My word, she doesn't know what she's letting herself in for,' said Banford, in her plaintive, drifting, insulting voice.

'What has it got to do with you, anyway?' said the youth, in a temper.

'More than it has to do with you, probably,' she replied, plaintive and venomous.

'Oh, has it! I don't see that at all,' he jerked out.

'No, you wouldn't,' she answered, drifting.

'Anyhow,' said March, pushing back her hair and rising uncouthly. 'It's no good arguing about it.' And she seized the bread and the tea-pot and strode away to the kitchen.

Banford let her fingers stray across her brow and along her hair, like one bemused. Then she turned and went away upstairs.

Henry sat stiff and sulky in his chair, with his face and his eyes on fire. March came and went, clearing the table. But Henry sat on, stiff with temper. He took no notice of her. She had regained her composure and her soft, even, creamy complexion. But her mouth was pursed up.

She glanced at him each time as she came to take things from the table, glanced from her large, curious eyes, more in curiosity than anything. Such a long, red-faced, sulky boy! That was all he was. He seemed as remote from her as if his red face were a red chimney-pot on a cottage across the fields, and she looked at him just as objectively, as remotely.

At length he got up and stalked out into the fields with the gun. He came in only at dinner-time, with the devil still in his face, but his manners quite polite. Nobody said anything particular; they sat each one at the sharp corner of a triangle, in obstinate remoteness. In the afternoon he went out again at once with the gun. He came in at nightfall with a rabbit and a pigeon. He stayed in all the evening, but hardly opened his mouth. He was in the devil of a temper, feeling he had been insulted.

Banford's eyes were red, she had evidently been crying. But her manner was more remote and supercilious than ever; the way she turned her head if he spoke at all, as if he were some tramp or inferior intruder of that sort, made his blue eyes go almost black with rage. His face looked sulkier. But he never forgot his polite intonation, if he opened his mouth to speak. March seemed to flourish in this atmosphere. She seemed to sit between the two antagonists with a little wicked smile on her face, enjoying herself. There was even a sort of complacency in the way she laboriously crocheted this evening.

When he was in bed, the youth could hear the two women talking and arguing in their room. He sat up in bed and strained his ears to hear what they said. But he could hear nothing, it was too far off. Yet he could hear the soft, plaintive drip of Banford's voice, and March's deeper note.

The night was quiet, frosty. Big stars were snapping outside, beyond the ridge-tops of the pine trees. He listened and listened. In the distance he heard a fox yelping: and the dogs from the farms barking in answer. But it was not that he wanted to hear. It was what the two women were saying.

He got stealthily out of bed and stood by his door. He could hear no more than before. Very, very carefully he began to lift the door latch. After quite a time he had his door open. Then he stepped stealthily out into the passage. The old oak planks were cold under his feet, and they creaked preposterously. He crept very, very gently up the one step, and along by the wall, till he stood outside their door. And there he held his breath and listened. Banford's voice:

'No, I simply couldn't stand it. I should be dead in a month. Which is just what he would be aiming at, of course. That would just be his game, to see me in the churchyard. No, Nellie, if you were to do such a thing as to marry him, you could never stop here. I couldn't, I couldn't live in the same house with him. Oh! - oh! I feel quite sick with the smell of his clothes. And his red face simply turns me over. I can't eat my food when he's at the table. What a fool I was ever to let him stop. One ought NEVER to try to do a kind action. It always flies back in your face like a boomerang.'

'Well, he's only got two more days,' said March.

'Yes, thank heaven. And when he's gone he'll never come in this house again. I feel so bad while he's here. And I know, I know he's only counting what he can get out of you. I KNOW that's all it is. He's just a good-for-nothing, who doesn't want to work, and who thinks he'll live on us. But he won't live on me. If you're such a fool, then it's your own lookout. Mrs Burgess knew him all the time he was here. And the old man could never get him to do any steady work. He was off with the gun on every occasion, just as he is now. Nothing but the gun! Oh, I do hate it. You don't know what you're doing, Nellie, you don't. If you marry him he'll just make a fool of you. He'll go off and leave you stranded. I know he will, if he can't get Bailey Farm out of us - and he's not going to, while I live. While I live he's never going to set foot here. I know what it would be. He'd soon think he was master of both of us, as he thinks he's master of you already.'

'But he isn't,' said Nellie.

'He thinks he is, anyway. And that's what he wants: to come and be master here. Yes, imagine it! That's what we've got the place together for, is it, to be bossed and bullied by a hateful, red-faced boy, a beastly labourer. Oh, we DID make a mistake when we let him stop. We ought never to have lowered ourselves. And I've had such a fight with all the people here, not to be pulled down to their level. No, he's not coming here. And then you see - if he can't have the place, he'll run off to Canada or somewhere again, as if he'd never known you. And here you'll be, absolutely ruined and made a fool of. I know I shall never have any peace of mind again.'

'We'll tell him he can't come here. We'll tell him that,' said March.

'Oh, don't you bother; I'm going to tell him that, and other things as well, before he goes. He's not going to have all his own way while I've got the strength left to speak. Oh, Nellie, he'll despise you, he'll despise you, like the awful little beast he is, if you give way to him. I'd no more trust him than I'd trust a cat not to steal. He's deep, he's deep, and he's bossy, and he's selfish through and through, as cold as ice. All he wants is to make use of you. And when you're no more use to him, then I pity you.'

'I don't think he's as bad as all that,' said March.

'No, because he's been playing up to you. But you'll find out, if you see much of him. Oh, Nellie, I can't bear to think of it.'

'Well, it won't hurt you, Jill, darling.'

'Won't it! Won't it! I shall never know a moment's peace again while I live, nor a moment's happiness. No, Nellie - ' and Banford began to weep bitterly.

The boy outside could hear the stifled sound of the woman's sobbing, and could hear March's soft, deep, tender voice comforting, with wonderful gentleness and tenderness, the weeping woman.

His eyes were so round and wide that he seemed to see the whole night, and his ears were almost jumping off his head. He was frozen stiff. He crept back to bed, but felt as if the top of his head were coming off. He could not sleep. He could not keep still. He rose, quietly dressed himself, and crept out on to the landing once more. The women were silent. He went softly downstairs and out to the kitchen.

Then he put on his boots and his overcoat and took the gun. He did not think to go away from the farm. No, he only took the gun. As softly as possible he unfastened the door and went out into the frosty December night. The air was still, the stars bright, the pine trees seemed to bristle audibly in the sky. He went stealthily away down a fence-side, looking for something to shoot. At the same time he remembered that he ought not to shoot and frighten the women.

So he prowled round the edge of the gorse cover, and through the grove of tall old hollies, to the woodside. There he skirted the fence, peering through the darkness with dilated eyes that seemed to be able to grow black and full of sight in the dark, like a cat's. An owl was slowly and mournfully whooing round a great oak tree. He stepped stealthily with his gun, listening, listening, watching.

As he stood under the oaks of the wood-edge he heard the dogs from the neighbouring cottage up the hill yelling suddenly and startlingly, and the wakened dogs from the farms around barking answer. And suddenly it seemed to him England was little and tight, he felt the landscape was constricted even in the dark, and that there were too many dogs in the night, making a noise like a fence of sound, like the network of English hedges netting the view. He felt the fox didn't have a chance. For it must be the fox that had started all this hullabaloo.

Why not watch for him, anyhow! He would, no doubt, be coming sniffing round. The lad walked downhill to where the farmstead with its few pine trees crouched blackly. In the angle of the long shed, in the black dark, he crouched down. He knew the fox would be coming. It seemed to him it would be the last of the foxes in this loudly-barking, thick-voiced England, tight with innumerable little houses.

He sat a long time with his eyes fixed unchanging upon the open gateway, where a little light seemed to fall from the stars or from the horizon, who knows. He was sitting on a log in a dark corner with the gun across his knees. The pine trees snapped. Once a chicken fell off its perch in the barn with a loud crawk and cackle and commotion that startled him, and he stood up, watching with all his eyes, thinking it might be a rat. But he FELT it was nothing. So he sat down again with the gun on his knees and his hands tucked in to keep them warm, and his eyes fixed unblinking on the pale reach of the open gateway. He felt he could smell the hot, sickly, rich smell of live chickens on the cold air.

And then - a shadow. A sliding shadow in the gateway. He gathered all his vision into a concentrated spark, and saw the shadow of the fox, the fox creeping on his belly through the gate. There he went, on his belly like a snake. The boy smiled to himself and brought the gun to his shoulder. He knew quite well what would happen. He knew the fox would go to where the fowl door was boarded up and sniff there. He knew he would lie there for a minute, sniffing the fowls within. And then he would start again prowling under the edge of the old barn, waiting to get in.

The fowl door was at the top of a slight incline. Soft, soft as a shadow the fox slid up this incline, and crouched with his nose to the boards. And at the same moment there was the awful crash of a gun

100

reverberating between the old buildings, as if all the night had gone smash. But the boy watched keenly. He saw even the white belly of the fox as the beast beat his paws in death. So he went forward.

There was a commotion everywhere. The fowls were scuffling and crawking, the ducks were quark-quarking, the pony had stamped wildly to his feet. But the fox was on his side, struggling in his last tremors. The boy bent over him and smelt his foxy smell.

There was a sound of a window opening upstairs, then March's voice calling:

'Who is it?'

'It's me,' said Henry; 'I've shot the fox.'

'Oh, goodness! You nearly frightened us to death.'

'Did I? I'm awfully sorry.'

'Whatever made you get up?'

'I heard him about.'

'And have you shot him?'

'Yes, he's here,' and the boy stood in the yard holding up the warm, dead brute. 'You can't see, can you? Wait a minute.' And he took his flash-light from his pocket and flashed it on to the dead animal. He was holding it by the brush. March saw, in the middle of the darkness, just the reddish fleece and the white belly and the white underneath of the pointed chin, and the queer, dangling paws. She did not know what to say.

'He's a beauty,' he said. 'He will make you a lovely fur.'

'You don't catch me wearing a fox fur,' she replied.

'Oh!' he said. And he switched off the light.

'Well, I should think you'll come in and go to bed again now,' she said.

'Probably I shall. What time is it?'

'What time is it, Jill?' called March's voice. It was a quarter to one.

That night March had another dream. She dreamed that Banford was dead, and that she, March, was sobbing her heart out. Then she had to put Banford into her coffin. And the coffin was the rough wood-box in which the bits of chopped wood were kept in the kitchen, by the fire. This was the coffin, and there was no other, and March was in agony and dazed bewilderment, looking for something to line the box with, something to make it soft with, something to cover up the poor, dead darling. Because she couldn't lay her in there just in her white, thin nightdress, in the horrible wood-box. So she hunted and hunted, and picked up thing after thing, and threw it aside in the agony of dream-frustration. And in her dream-despair all she could find that would do was a fox-skin. She knew that it wasn't right, that this was not what she should have. But it was all she could find. And so she folded the brush of the fox, and laid her darling Jill's head on this, and she brought round the skin of the fox and laid it on the top of the body, so that it seemed to make a whole ruddy, fiery coverlet, and she cried and cried, and woke to find the tears streaming down her face.

The first thing that both she and Banford did in the morning was to go out to see the fox. Henry had hung it up by the heels in the shed, with its poor brush falling backwards. It was a lovely dog-fox in its prime, with a handsome, thick, winter coat: a lovely golden-red colour, with grey as it passed to the belly, and belly all white, and a great full brush with a delicate black and grey and pure white tip.

'Poor brute!' said Banford. 'If it wasn't such a thieving wretch, you'd feel sorry for it.'

March said nothing, but stood with her foot trailing aside, one hip out; her face was pale and her eyes big and black, watching the dead animal that was suspended upside down. White and soft as snow his belly: white and soft as snow. She passed her hand softly down it. And his wonderful black-glinted brush was full and frictional, wonderful. She passed her hand down this also, and quivered. Time after time she took the full fur of that thick tail between her fingers, and passed her hand slowly downwards. Wonderful, sharp, thick, splendour of a tail. And he was dead! She pursed her lips, and her eyes went black and vacant. Then she took the head in her hand.

Henry was sauntering up, so Banford walked rather pointedly away. March stood there bemused, with the head of the fox in her hand. She was wondering, wondering, wondering over his long, fine muzzle. For some reason it reminded her of a spoon or a spatula. She felt she could not understand it. The beast was a strange beast to her, incomprehensible, out of her range. Wonderful silver whiskers he had, like ice-threads. And pricked ears with hair inside. But that long, long, slender spoon of a nose! - and the marvellous white teeth beneath! It was to thrust forward and bite with, deep, deep, deep into the living prey, to bite and bite the blood.

'He's a beauty, isn't he?' said Henry, standing by.

'Oh yes, he's a fine big fox. I wonder how many chickens he's responsible for,' she replied.

'A good many. Do you think he's the same one you saw in the summer?'

'I should think very likely he is,' she replied.

He watched her, but he could make nothing of her. Partly she was so shy and virgin, and partly she was so grim, matter-of-fact, shrewish. What she said seemed to him so different from the look of her big, queer, dark eyes.

'Are you going to skin him?' she asked.

'Yes, when I've had breakfast, and got a board to peg him on.'

'My word, what a strong smell he's got! Pooo! It'll take some washing off one's hands. I don't know why I was so silly as to handle him.' And she looked at her right hand, that had passed down his belly and along his tail, and had even got a tiny streak of blood from one dark place in his fur.

'Have you seen the chickens when they smell him, how frightened they are?' he said.

'Yes, aren't they!'

'You must mind you don't get some of his fleas.'

'Oh, fleas!' she replied, nonchalant.

Later in the day she saw the fox's skin nailed flat on a board, as if crucified. It gave her an uneasy feeling.

The boy was angry. He went about with his mouth shut, as if he had swallowed part of his chin. But in behaviour he was polite and affable. He did not say anything about his intention. And he left March alone.

That evening they sat in the dining-room. Banford wouldn't have him in her sitting-room any more. There was a very big log on the fire. And everybody was busy. Banford had letters to write. March was sewing a dress, and he was mending some little contrivance.

Banford stopped her letter-writing from time to time to look round and rest her eyes. The boy had his head down, his face hidden over his job.

'Let's see,' said Banford. 'What train do you go by, Henry?'

He looked up straight at her.

'The morning train. In the morning,' he said.

'What, the eight-ten or the eleven-twenty?'

'The eleven-twenty, I suppose,' he said.

'That is the day after tomorrow?' said Banford.

'Yes, the day after tomorrow.'

'Mm!' murmured Banford, and she returned to her writing. But as she was licking her envelope, she asked:

'And what plans have you made for the future, if I may ask?'

'Plans?' he said, his face very bright and angry.

'I mean about you and Nellie, if you are going on with this business. When do you expect the wedding to come off?' She spoke in a jeering tone.

'Oh, the wedding!' he replied. 'I don't know.'

'Don't you know anything?' said Banford. 'Are you going to clear out on Friday and leave things no more settled than they are?'

'Well, why shouldn't I? We can always write letters.'

'Yes, of course you can. But I wanted to know because of this place. If Nellie is going to get married all of a sudden, I shall have to be looking round for a new partner.'

'Couldn't she stay on here if she were married?' he said. He knew quite well what was coming.

'Oh,' said Banford, 'this is no place for a married couple. There's not enough work to keep a man going, for one thing. And there's no money to be made. It's quite useless your thinking of staying on here if you marry. Absolutely!'

'Yes, but I wasn't thinking of staying on here,' he said.

'Well, that's what I want to know. And what about Nellie, then? How long is SHE going to be here with me, in that case?'

The two antagonists looked at one another.

'That I can't say,' he answered.

'Oh, go along,' she cried petulantly. 'You must have some idea what you are going to do, if you ask a woman to marry you. Unless it's all a hoax.'

'Why should it be a hoax? I am going back to Canada.'

'And taking her with you?'

'Yes, certainly.'

'You hear that, Nellie?' said Banford.

March, who had had her head bent over her sewing, now looked up with a sharp, pink blush on her face, and a queer, sardonic laugh in her eyes and on her twisted mouth.

'That's the first time I've heard that I was going to Canada,' she said.

'Well, you have to hear it for the first time, haven't you?' said the boy.

'Yes, I suppose I have,' she said nonchalantly. And she went back to her sewing.

'You're quite ready, are you, to go to Canada? Are you, Nellie?' asked Banford.

March looked up again. She let her shoulders go slack, and let her hand that held the needle lie loose in her lap.

'It depends on HOW I'm going,' she said. 'I don't think I want to go jammed up in the steerage, as a soldier's wife. I'm afraid I'm not used to that way.'

The boy watched her with bright eyes.

'Would you rather stay over here while I go first?' he asked.

'I would, if that's the only alternative,' she replied.

'That's much the wisest. Don't make it any fixed engagement,' said Banford. 'Leave yourself free to go or not after he's got back and found you a place, Nellie. Anything else is madness, madness.'

'Don't you think,' said the youth, 'we ought to get married before I go - and then go together, or separate, according to how it happens?'

'I think it's a terrible idea,' cried Banford.

But the boy was watching March.

'What do you think?' he asked her.

She let her eyes stray vaguely into space.

'Well, I don't know,' she said. 'I shall have to think about it.'

'Why?' he asked pertinently.

'Why?' She repeated his question in a mocking way and looked at him laughing, though her face was pink again. 'I should think there's plenty of reasons why.'

He watched her in silence. She seemed to have escaped him. She had got into league with Banford against him. There was again the queer, sardonic look about her; she would mock stoically at everything he said or which life offered.

'Of course,' he said, 'I don't want to press you to do anything you don't wish to do.'

'I should think not, indeed,' cried Banford indignantly.

At bed-time Banford said plaintively to March:

'You take my hot bottle up for me, Nellie, will you?'

'Yes, I'll do it,' said March, with the kind of willing unwillingness she so often showed towards her beloved but uncertain Jill.

The two women went upstairs. After a time March called from the top of the stairs: 'Good-night, Henry. I shan't be coming down. You'll see to the lamp and the fire, won't you?'

The next day Henry went about with the cloud on his brow and his young cub's face shut up tight. He was cogitating all the time. He had wanted March to marry him and go back to Canada with him. And he had been sure she would do it. Why he wanted her he didn't know. But he did want her. He had set his mind on her. And he was convulsed with a youth's fury at being thwarted. To be thwarted, to be thwarted! It made him so furious inside that he did not know what to do with himself. But he kept himself in hand. Because even now things might turn out differently. She might come over to him. Of course she might. It was her business to do so.

Things drew to a tension again towards evening. He and Banford had avoided each other all day. In fact, Banford went in to the little town by the 11.20 train. It was market day. She arrived back on the 4.25. Just as the night was falling Henry saw her little figure in a dark-blue coat and a dark-blue tam-o'-shanter hat crossing the first meadow from the station. He stood under one of the wild pear trees, with the old dead leaves round his feet. And he watched the little blue figure advancing persistently over the rough winter-ragged meadow. She had her arms full of parcels, and advanced slowly, frail thing she was, but with that devilish little certainty which he so detested in her. He stood invisible under the pear tree, watching her every step.

And if looks could have affected her, she would have felt a log of iron on each of her ankles as she made her way forward. 'You're a nasty little thing, you are,' he was saying softly, across the distance. 'You're a nasty little thing. I hope you'll be paid back for all the harm you've done me for nothing. I hope you will - you nasty little thing. I hope you'll have to pay for it. You will, if wishes are anything. You nasty little creature that you are.'

She was toiling slowly up the slope. But if she had been slipping back at every step towards the Bottomless Pit, he would not have gone to help her with her parcels. Aha, there went March, striding with her long, land stride in her breeches and her short tunic! Striding downhill at a great pace, and even running a few steps now and then, in her great solicitude and desire to come to the rescue of the little Banford. The boy watched her with rage in his heart. See her leap a ditch, and run, run as if a house was on fire, just to get to that creeping, dark little object down there! So, the Banford just stood still and waited. And March strode up and took ALL the parcels except a bunch of yellow chrysanthemums. These the Banford still carried - yellow chrysanthemums!

'Yes, you look well, don't you?' he said softly into the dusk air. 'You look well, pottering up there with a bunch of flowers, you do. I'd make you eat them for your tea if you hug them so tight. And I'd give them you for breakfast again, I would. I'd give you flowers. Nothing but flowers.'

He watched the progress of the two women. He could hear their voices: March always outspoken and rather scolding in her tenderness, Banford murmuring rather vaguely. They were evidently good friends. He could not hear what they said till they came to the fence of the home meadow, which they must climb. Then he saw March manfully climbing over the bars with all her packages in her arms, and on the still air he heard Banford's fretful:

'Why don't you let me help you with the parcels?' She had a queer, plaintive hitch in her voice. Then came March's robust and reckless:

'Oh, I can manage. Don't you bother about me. You've all you can do to get yourself over.'

'Yes, that's all very well,' said Banford fretfully. 'You say, Don't you bother about me, and then all the while you feel injured because nobody thinks of you.'

'When do I feel injured?' said March.

'Always. You always feel injured. Now you're feeling injured because I won't have that boy to come and live on the farm.'

'I'm not feeling injured at all,' said March. 'I know you are. When he's gone you'll sulk over it. I know you will.'

'Shall I?' said March. 'We'll see.'

'Yes, we SHALL see, unfortunately. I can't think how you can make yourself so cheap. I can't IMAGINE how you can lower yourself like it.'

'I haven't lowered myself,' said March.

'I don't know what you call it, then. Letting a boy like that come so cheeky and impudent and make a mug of you. I don't know what you think of yourself. How much respect do you think he's going to have for you afterwards? My word, I wouldn't be in your shoes, if you married him.'

'Of course you wouldn't. My boots are a good bit too big for you, and not half dainty enough,' said March, with rather a misfire sarcasm.

'I thought you had too much pride, really I did. A woman's got to hold herself high, especially with a youth like that. Why, he's impudent. Even the way he forced himself on us at the start.'

'We asked him to stay,' said March.

'Not till he'd almost forced us to. And then he's so cocky and self-assured. My word, he puts my back up. I simply can't imagine how you can let him treat you so cheaply.'

'I don't let him treat me cheaply,' said March. 'Don't you worry yourself, nobody's going to treat me cheaply. And even you aren't, either.' She had a tender defiance and a certain fire in her voice.

'Yes, it's sure to come back to me,' said Banford bitterly. 'That's always the end of it. I believe you only do it to spite me.'

They went now in silence up the steep, grassy slope and over the brow, through the gorse bushes. On the other side of the hedge the boy followed in the dusk, at some little distance. Now and then, through the huge ancient hedge of hawthorn, risen into trees, he saw the two dark figures creeping up the hill. As he came to the top of the slope he saw the homestead dark in the twilight, with a huge old pear tree leaning from the near gable, and a little yellow light twinkling in the small side windows of the kitchen. He heard the clink of the latch and saw the kitchen door open into light as the two women went indoors. So they were at home.

And so! - this was what they thought of him. It was rather in his nature to be a listener, so he was not at all surprised whatever he heard. The things people said about him always missed him personally. He was only rather surprised at the women's way with one another. And he disliked the Banford with an acid dislike. And he felt drawn to the March again. He felt again irresistibly drawn to her. He felt there was a secret bond, a secret thread between him and her, something very

108

exclusive, which shut out everybody else and made him and her possess each other in secret.

He hoped again that she would have him. He hoped with his blood suddenly firing up that she would agree to marry him quite quickly: at Christmas, very likely. Christmas was not far off. He wanted, whatever else happened, to snatch her into a hasty marriage and a consummation with him. Then for the future, they could arrange later. But he hoped it would happen as he wanted it. He hoped that tonight she would stay a little while with him, after Banford had gone upstairs. He hoped he could touch her soft, creamy cheek, her strange, frightened face. He hoped he could look into her dilated, frightened dark eyes, quite near. He hoped he might even put his hand on her bosom and feel her soft breasts under her tunic. His heart beat deep and powerful as he thought of that. He wanted very much to do so. He wanted to make sure of her soft woman's breasts under her tunic. She always kept the brown linen coat buttoned so close up to her throat. It seemed to him like some perilous secret, that her soft woman's breasts must be buttoned up in that uniform. It seemed to him, moreover, that they were so much softer, tenderer, more lovely and lovable, shut up in that tunic, than were the Banford's breasts, under her soft blouses and chiffon dresses. The Banford would have little iron breasts, he said to himself. For all her frailty and fretfulness and delicacy, she would have tiny iron breasts. But March, under her crude, fast, workman's tunic, would have soft, white breasts, white and unseen. So he told himself, and his blood burned.

When he went in to tea, he had a surprise. He appeared at the inner door, his face very ruddy and vivid and his blue eyes shining, dropping his head forward as he came in, in his usual way, and hesitating in the doorway to watch the inside of the room, keenly and cautiously, before he entered. He was wearing a long-sleeved waistcoat. His face seemed extraordinarily like a piece of the out-of-doors come indoors: as holly-berries do. In his second of pause in the doorway he took in the two women sitting at table, at opposite ends, saw them sharply. And to his amazement March was dressed in a dress of dull, green silk crape. His mouth came open in surprise. If she had suddenly grown a moustache he could not have been more surprised.

'Why,' he said, 'do you wear a dress, then?'

She looked up, flushing a deep rose colour, and twisting her mouth with a smile, said:

'Of course I do. What else do you expect me to wear but a dress?'

'A land girl's uniform, of course,' said he.

'Oh,' she cried, nonchalant, 'that's only for this dirty, mucky work about here.'

'Isn't it your proper dress, then?' he said.

'No, not indoors it isn't,' she said. But she was blushing all the time as she poured out his tea. He sat down in his chair at table, unable to take his eyes off her. Her dress was a perfectly simple slip of bluey-green crape, with a line of gold stitching round the top and round the sleeves, which came to the elbow. It was cut just plain and round at the top, and showed her white, soft throat. Her arms he knew, strong and firm muscled, for he had often seen her with her sleeves rolled up. But he looked her up and down, up and down,

Banford, at the other end of the table, said not a word, but piggled with the sardine on her plate. He had forgotten her existence. He just simply stared at March while he ate his bread and margarine in huge mouthfuls, forgetting even his tea.

'Well, I never knew anything make such a difference!' he murmured, across his mouthfuls.

'Oh, goodness!' cried March, blushing still more. 'I might be a pink monkey!'

And she rose quickly to her feet and took the tea-pot to the fire, to the kettle. And as she crouched on the hearth with her green slip about her, the boy stared more wide-eyed than ever. Through the crape her woman's form seemed soft and womanly. And when she stood up and walked he saw her legs move soft within her modernly short skirt. She had on black silk stockings, and small patent shoes with little gold buckles.

No, she was another being. She was something quite different. Seeing her always in the hard-cloth breeches, wide on the hips, buttoned on the knee, strong as armour, and in the brown puttees and thick boots, it had never occurred to him that she had a woman's legs and feet. Now it came upon him. She had a woman's soft, skirted legs, and she was accessible. He blushed to the roots of his hair, shoved his nose in his tea-cup and drank his tea with a little noise that made

110

Banford simply squirm: and strangely, suddenly he felt a man, no longer a youth. He felt a man, with all a man's grave weight of responsibility. A curious quietness and gravity came over his soul. He felt a man, quiet, with a little of the heaviness of male destiny upon him.

She was soft and accessible in her dress. The thought went home in him like an everlasting responsibility.

'Oh, for goodness' sake, say something, somebody,' cried Banford fretfully. 'It might be a funeral.' The boy looked at her, and she could not bear his face.

'A funeral!' said March, with a twisted smile. 'Why, that breaks my dream.'

Suddenly she had thought of Banford in the wood-box for a coffin.

'What, have you been dreaming of a wedding?' said Banford sarcastically.

'Must have been,' said March.

'Whose wedding?' asked the boy.

'I can't remember,' said March.

She was shy and rather awkward that evening, in spite of the fact that, wearing a dress, her bearing was much more subdued than in her uniform. She felt unpeeled and rather exposed. She felt almost improper.

They talked desultorily about Henry's departure next morning, and made the trivial arrangement. But of the matter on their minds, none of them spoke. They were rather quiet and friendly this evening; Banford had practically nothing to say. But inside herself she seemed still, perhaps kindly.

At nine o'clock March brought in the tray with the everlasting tea and a little cold meat which Banford had managed to procure. It was the last supper, so Banford did not want to be disagreeable. She felt a bit sorry for the boy, and felt she must be as nice as she could.

He wanted her to go to bed. She was usually the first. But she sat on in her chair under the lamp, glancing at her book now and then, and staring into the fire. A deep silence had come into the room. It was broken by March asking, in a rather small tone:

'What time is it, Jill?'

'Five past ten,' said Banford, looking at her wrist.

And then not a sound. The boy had looked up from the book he was holding between his knees. His rather wide, cat-shaped face had its obstinate look, his eyes were watchful.

'What about bed?' said March at last.

'I'm ready when you are,' said Banford.

'Oh, very well,' said March. 'I'll fill your bottle.'

She was as good as her word. When the hot-water bottle was ready, she lit a candle and went upstairs with it. Banford remained in her chair, listening acutely. March came downstairs again.

'There you are, then,' she said. 'Are you going up?'

'Yes, in a minute,' said Banford. But the minute passed, and she sat on in her chair under the lamp.

Henry, whose eyes were shining like a cat's as he watched from under his brows, and whose face seemed wider, more chubbed and cat-like with unalterable obstinacy, now rose to his feet to try his throw.

'I think I'll go and look if I can see the she-fox,' he said. 'She may be creeping round. Won't you come as well for a minute, Nellie, and see if we see anything?'

'Me!' cried March, looking up with her startled, wondering face.

'Yes. Come on,' he said. It was wonderful how soft and warm and coaxing his voice could be, how near. The very sound of it made Banford's blood boil. 'Come on for a minute,' he said, looking down into her uplifted, unsure face.

And she rose to her feet as if drawn up by his young, ruddy face that was looking down on her.

'I should think you're never going out at this time of night, Nellie!' cried Banford.

'Yes, just for a minute,' said the boy, looking round on her, and speaking with an odd, sharp yelp in his voice.

March looked from one to the other, as if confused, vague. Banford rose to her feet for battle.

'Why, it's ridiculous. It's bitter cold. You'll catch your death in that thin frock. And in those slippers. You're not going to do any such thing.'

There was a moment's pause. Banford turtled up like a little fighting cock, facing March and the boy.

'Oh, I don't think you need worry yourself,' he replied. 'A moment under the stars won't do anybody any damage. I'll get the rug off the sofa in the dining-room. You're coming, Nellie.'

His voice had so much anger and contempt and fury in it as he spoke to Banford: and so much tenderness and proud authority as he spoke to March, that the latter answered:

'Yes, I'm coming.'

And she turned with him to the door.

Banford, standing there in the middle of the room, suddenly burst into a long wail and a spasm of sobs. She covered her face with her poor, thin hands, and her thin shoulders shook in an agony of weeping. March looked back from the door.

'Jill!' she cried in a frantic tone, like someone just coming awake. And she seemed to start towards her darling.

But the boy had March's arm in his grip, and she could not move. She did not know why she could not move. It was as in a dream when the heart strains and the body cannot stir.

'Never mind,' said the boy softly. 'Let her cry. Let her cry. She will have to cry sooner or later. And the tears will relieve her feelings. They will do her good.'

So he drew March slowly through the doorway. But her last look was back to the poor little figure which stood in the middle of the room with covered face and thin shoulders shaken with bitter weeping.

In the dining-room he picked up the rug and said:

'Wrap yourself up in this.'

She obeyed - and they reached the kitchen door, he holding her soft and firm by the arm, though she did not know it. When she saw the night outside she started back.

'I must go back to Jill,' she said. 'I MUST! Oh yes, I must.'

Her tone sounded final. The boy let go of her and she turned indoors. But he seized her again and arrested her.

'Wait a minute,' he said. 'Wait a minute. Even if you go, you're not going yet.'

'Leave go! Leave go!' she cried. 'My place is at Jill's side. Poor little thing, she's sobbing her heart out.'

'Yes,' said the boy bitterly. 'And your heart too, and mine as well.'

'Your heart?' said March. He still gripped her and detained her.

'Isn't it as good as her heart?' he said. 'Or do you think it's not?'

'Your heart?' she said again, incredulous.

'Yes, mine! Mine! Do you think I haven't GOT a heart?' And with his hot grasp he took her hand and pressed it under his left breast. 'There's my heart,' he said, 'if you don't believe in it.'

It was wonder which made her attend. And then she felt the deep, heavy, powerful stroke of his heart, terrible, like something from beyond. It was like something from beyond, something awful from outside, signalling to her. And the signal paralysed her. It beat upon her very soul, and made her helpless. She forgot Jill. She could not think of Jill any more. She could not think of her. That terrible signalling from outside!

The boy put his arm round her waist.

'Come with me,' he said gently. 'Come and let us say what we've got to say.'

And he drew her outside, closed the door. And she went with him darkly down the garden path. That he should have a beating heart! And that he should have his arm round her, outside the blanket! She was too confused to think who he was or what he was.

He took her to a dark corner of the shed, where there was a tool-box with a lid, long and low.

'We'll sit here a minute,' he said.

And obediently she sat down by his side.

'Give me your hand,' he said.

She gave him both her hands, and he held them between his own. He was young, and it made him tremble.

'You'll marry me. You'll marry me before I go back, won't you?' he pleaded.

'Why, aren't we both a pair of fools?' she said.

He had put her in the corner, so that she should not look out and see the lighted window of the house across the dark garden. He tried to keep her all there inside the shed with him.

'In what way a pair of fools?' he said. 'If you go back to Canada with me, I've got a job and a good wage waiting for me, and it's a nice place, near the mountains. Why shouldn't you marry me? Why shouldn't we marry? I should like to have you there with me. I should like to feel I'd got somebody there, at the back of me, all my life.'

'You'd easily find somebody else who'd suit you better,' she said.

114

'Yes, I might easily find another girl. I know I could. But not one I really wanted. I've never met one I really wanted for good. You see, I'm thinking of all my life. If I marry, I want to feel it's for all my life. Other girls: well, they're just girls, nice enough to go a walk with now and then. Nice enough for a bit of play. But when I think of my life, then I should be very sorry to have to marry one of them, I should indeed.'

'You mean they wouldn't make you a good wife.'

'Yes, I mean that. But I don't mean they wouldn't do their duty by me. I mean - I don't know what I mean. Only when I think of my life, and of you, then the two things go together.'

'And what if they didn't?' she said, with her odd, sardonic touch.

'Well, I think they would.'

They sat for some time silent. He held her hands in his, but he did not make love to her. Since he had realized that she was a woman, and vulnerable, accessible, a certain heaviness had possessed his soul. He did not want to make love to her. He shrank from any such performance, almost with fear. She was a woman, and vulnerable, accessible to him finally, and he held back from that which was ahead, almost with dread. It was a kind of darkness he knew he would enter finally, but of which he did not want as yet even to think. She was the woman, and he was responsible for the strange vulnerability he had suddenly realized in her.

'No,' she said at last, 'I'm a fool. I know I'm a fool.'

'What for?' he asked.

'To go on with this business.'

'Do you mean me?' he asked.

'No, I mean myself. I'm making a fool of myself, and a big one.'

'Why, because you don't want to marry me, really?'

'Oh, I don't know whether I'm against it, as a matter of fact. That's just it. I don't know.'

He looked at her in the darkness, puzzled. He did not in the least know what she meant.

'And don't you know whether you like to sit here with me this minute or not?' he asked.

'No, I don't really. I don't know whether I wish I was somewhere else, or whether I like being here. I don't know, really.'

'Do you wish you were with Miss Banford? Do you wish you'd gone to bed with her?' he asked, as a challenge.

She waited a long time before she answered:

'No,' she said at last. 'I don't wish that.'

'And do you think you would spend all your life with her - when your hair goes white, and you are old?' he said.

'No,' she said, without much hesitation. 'I don't see Jill and me two old women together.'

'And don't you think, when I'm an old man and you're an old woman, we might be together still, as we are now?' he said.

'Well, not as we are now,' she replied. 'But I could imagine - no, I can't. I can't imagine you an old man. Besides, it's dreadful!'

'What, to be an old man?'

'Yes, of course.'

'Not when the time comes,' he said. 'But it hasn't come. Only it will. And when it does, I should like to think you'd be there as well.'

'Sort of old age pensions,' she said dryly.

Her kind of witless humour always startled him. He never knew what she meant. Probably she didn't quite know herself.

'No,' he said, hurt.

'I don't know why you harp on old age,' she said. 'I'm not ninety.'

'Did anybody ever say you were?' he asked, offended.

They were silent for some time, pulling different ways in the silence.

'I don't want you to make fun of me,' he said.

'Don't you?' she replied, enigmatic.

'No, because just this minute I'm serious. And when I'm serious, I believe in not making fun of it.'

'You mean nobody else must make fun of you,' she replied.

'Yes, I mean that. And I mean I don't believe in making fun of it myself. When it comes over me so that I'm serious, then - there it is, I don't want it to be laughed at.'

She was silent for some time. Then she said, in a vague, almost pained voice:

'No, I'm not laughing at you.'

A hot wave rose in his heart.

'You believe me, do you?' he asked.

'Yes, I believe you,' she replied, with a twang of her old, tired

116

nonchalance, as if she gave in because she was tired. But he didn't care. His heart was hot and clamorous.

'So you agree to marry me before I go? - perhaps at Christmas?'

'Yes, I agree.'

'There!' he exclaimed. 'That's settled it.'

And he sat silent, unconscious, with all the blood burning in all his veins, like fire in all the branches and twigs of him. He only pressed her two hands to his chest, without knowing. When the curious passion began to die down, he seemed to come awake to the world.

'We'll go in, shall we?' he said: as if he realized it was cold.

She rose without answering.

'Kiss me before we go, now you've said it,' he said.

And he kissed her gently on the mouth, with a young, frightened kiss. It made her feel so young, too, and frightened, and wondering: and tired, tired, as if she were going to sleep.

They went indoors. And in the sitting-room, there, crouched by the fire like a queer little witch, was Banford. She looked round with reddened eyes as they entered, but did not rise. He thought she looked frightening, unnatural, crouching there and looking round at them. Evil he thought her look was, and he crossed his fingers.

Banford saw the ruddy, elate face on the youth: he seemed strangely tall and bright and looming. And March had a delicate look on her face; she wanted to hide her face, to screen it, to let it not be seen.

'You've come at last,' said Banford uglily.

'Yes, we've come,' said he.

'You've been long enough for anything,' she said.

'Yes, we have. We've settled it. We shall marry as soon as possible,' he replied.

'Oh, you've settled it, have you! Well, I hope you won't live to repent it,' said Banford.

'I hope so too,' he replied.

'Are you going to bed NOW, Nellie?' said Banford.

'Yes, I'm going now.'

'Then for goodness' sake come along.'

March looked at the boy. He was glancing with his very bright eyes at her and at Banford. March looked at him wistfully. She wished she could stay with him. She wished she had married him already, and it was all over. For oh, she felt suddenly so safe with him. She felt so strangely safe and peaceful in his presence. If only she could sleep in his shelter, and not with Jill. She felt afraid of Jill. In her dim, tender state, it was agony to have to go with Jill and sleep with her. She wanted the boy to save her. She looked again at him.

And he, watching with bright eyes, divined something of what she felt. It puzzled and distressed him that she must go with Jill.

'I shan't forget what you've promised,' he said, looking clear into her eyes, right into her eyes, so that he seemed to occupy all herself with his queer, bright look.

She smiled to him faintly, gently. She felt safe again - safe with him.

But in spite of all the boy's precautions, he had a setback. The morning he was leaving the farm he got March to accompany him to the market-town, about six miles away, where they went to the registrar and had their names stuck up as two people who were going to marry. He was to come at Christmas, and the wedding was to take place then. He hoped in the spring to be able to take March back to Canada with him, now the war was really over. Though he was so young, he had saved some money.

'You never have to be without SOME money at the back of you, if you can help it,' he said.

So she saw him off in the train that was going West: his camp was on Salisbury Plain. And with big, dark eyes she watched him go, and it seemed as if everything real in life was retreating as the train retreated with his queer, chubby, ruddy face, that seemed so broad across the cheeks, and which never seemed to change its expression, save when a cloud of sulky anger hung on the brow, or the bright eyes fixed themselves in their stare. This was what happened now. He leaned there out of the carriage window as the train drew off, saying good-bye and staring back at her, but his face quite unchanged. There was no emotion on his face. Only his eyes tightened and became fixed and intent in their watching like a cat's when suddenly she sees something and stares. So the boy's eyes stared fixedly as the train drew away, and she was left feeling intensely forlorn. Failing his physical presence, she seemed to have nothing of him. And she had nothing of anything. Only his face was fixed in her mind: the full, ruddy, unchanging cheeks, and the straight snout of a nose and the two eyes staring above. All she could remember was how he suddenly wrinkled his nose when he laughed, as a puppy does when he is playfully growling. But him, himself, and what he was - she knew nothing, she had nothing of him when he left her.

On the ninth day after he had left her he received this letter.

Dear Henry,

I have been over it all again in my mind, this business of me and you, and it seems to me impossible. When you aren't there I see what a fool I am. When you are there you seem to blind me to things as they actually are. You make me see things all unreal, and I don't know what. Then when I am alone again with Jill I seem to come to my own senses and realise what a fool I am making of myself, and how I am treating you unfairly. Because it must be unfair to you for me to go on with this affair when I can't feel in my heart that I really love you. I know people talk a lot of stuff and nonsense about love, and I don't want to do that. I want to keep to plain facts and act in a sensible way. And that seems to me what I'm not doing. I don't see on what grounds I am going to marry you. I know I am not head over heels in love with you, as I have fancied myself to be with fellows when I was a young fool of a girl. You are an absolute stranger to me, and it seems to me you will always be one. So on what grounds am I going to marry you? When I think of Jill, she is ten times more real to me. I know her and I'm awfully fond of her, and I hate myself for a beast if I ever hurt her little finger. We have a life together. And even if it can't last for ever, it is a life while it does last. And it might last as long as either of us lives. Who knows how long we've got to live? She is a delicate little thing, perhaps nobody but me knows how delicate. And as for me, I feel I might fall down the well any day. What I don't seem to see at all is you. When I think of what I've been and what I've done with you, I'm afraid I am a few screws loose. I should be sorry to think that softening of the brain is setting in so soon, but that is what it seems like. You are such an absolute stranger, and so different from what I'm used to, and we don't seem to have a thing in common. As for love, the very word seems impossible. I know what love means even in Jill's case, and I know that in this affair with you it's an absolute impossibility. And then going to Canada. I'm sure I must have been clean off my chump when I promised such a thing. It makes me feel fairly frightened of myself. I feel I might do something really silly that I wasn't responsible for - and end my days in a lunatic asylum. You may think that's all I'm fit for after the way I've gone on, but it isn't a very nice thought for me. Thank goodness Jill is here, and her being here makes me feel sane again, else I don't know what I might do; I might have an accident with the gun one evening. I love Jill, and she makes me feel safe and sane, with her loving anger against me for being such a fool. Well, what I want to say is, won't you let us cry the whole thing off? I can't marry you, and really, I won't do such a thing if it seems to me wrong. It is all a great mistake. I've made a complete fool of myself, and all I can do is to apologise to you and ask you please to forget it, and please to take no further notice of me. Your fox-skin is nearly ready, and seems all right, I will post it to you if you will let me know if this address is still right, and if you will accept my apology for the awful and lunatic way I have behaved with you, and then let the matter rest.

Jill sends her kindest regards. Her mother and father are staying with us over Christmas,

Yours very sincerely,

ELLEN MARCH.

The boy read this letter in camp as he was cleaning his kit. He set his teeth, and for a moment went almost pale, yellow round the eyes with fury. He said nothing and saw nothing and felt nothing but a livid rage that was quite unreasoning. Balked! Balked again! Balked! He wanted the woman, he had fixed like doom upon having her. He felt that was his doom, his destiny, and his reward, to have this woman. She was his heaven and hell on earth, and he would have none elsewhere. Sightless with rage and thwarted madness he got through the morning. Save that in his mind he was lurking and scheming towards an issue, he would have committed some insane act. Deep in himself he felt like roaring and howling and gnashing his teeth and breaking things. But he was too intelligent. He knew society was on top of him, and he must scheme. So with his teeth bitten together, and his nose curiously slightly lifted, like some creature that is vicious, and his eyes fixed and staring, he went through the morning's affairs drunk with anger and suppression. In his mind was one thing - Banford. He took no heed of all March's outpouring: none. One thorn rankled, stuck in his mind. Banford. In his mind, in his soul, in his whole being, one thorn rankling to insanity. And he would have to get it out. He would have to get the thorn of Banford out of his life, if he died for it.

With this one fixed idea in his mind, he went to ask for twenty-four hours' leave of absence. He knew it was not due to him. His consciousness was supernaturally keen. He knew where he must go - he must go to the captain. But how could he get at the captain? In that great camp of wooden huts and tents he had no idea where his captain was.

But he went to the officers' canteen. There was his captain standing talking with three other officers. Henry stood in the doorway at attention.

'May I speak to Captain Berryman?' The captain was Cornish like himself.

'What do you want?' called the captain.

'May I speak to you, Captain?'

'What do you want?' replied the captain, not stirring from among his group of fellow officers.

Henry watched his superior for a minute without speaking.

'You won't refuse me, sir, will you?' he asked gravely.

'It depends what it is.'

'Can I have twenty-four hours' leave?'

'No, you've no business to ask.'

'I know I haven't. But I must ask you.'

'You've had your answer.'

'Don't send me away, Captain.'

There was something strange about the boy as he stood there so everlasting in the doorway. The Cornish captain felt the strangeness at once, and eyed him shrewdly.

'Why, what's afoot?' he said, curious.

'I'm in trouble about something. I must go to Blewbury,' said the boy.

'Blewbury, eh? After the girls?'

'Yes, it is a woman, Captain.' And the boy, as he stood there with his head reaching forward a little, went suddenly terribly pale, or yellow, and his lips seemed to give off pain. The captain saw and paled a little also. He turned aside.

'Go on, then,' he said. 'But for God's sake don't cause any trouble of any sort.'

'I won't, Captain, thank you.'

He was gone. The captain, upset, took a gin and bitters. Henry managed to hire a bicycle. It was twelve o'clock when he left the camp. He had sixty miles of wet and muddy crossroads to ride. But he was in the saddle and down the road without a thought of food.

At the farm, March was busy with a work she had had some time in hand. A bunch of Scotch fir trees stood at the end of the open shed, on a little bank where ran the fence between two of the gorse-shaggy meadows. The farthest of these trees was dead - it had died in the summer, and stood with all its needles brown and sere in the air. It was not a very big tree. And it was absolutely dead. So March determined to have it, although they were not allowed to cut any of the timber. But it would make such splendid firing, in these days of scarce fuel.

She had been giving a few stealthy chops at the trunk for a week or more, every now and then hacking away for five minutes, low down, near the ground, so no one should notice. She had not tried the saw, it was such hard work, alone. Now the tree stood with a great yawning gap in his base, perched, as it were, on one sinew, and ready to fall. But he did not fall.

It was late in the damp December afternoon, with cold mists creeping out of the woods and up the hollows, and darkness waiting to sink in from above. There was a bit of yellowness where the sun was fading away beyond the low woods of the distance. March took her axe and went to the tree. The small thud-thud of her blows resounded rather ineffectual about the wintry homestead. Banford came out wearing her thick coat, but with no hat on her head, so that her thin, bobbed hair blew on the uneasy wind that sounded in the pines and in the wood.

'What I'm afraid of,' said Banford, 'is that it will fall on the shed and we sh'll have another job repairing that.'

'Oh, I don't think so,' said March, straightening herself and wiping her arm over her hot brow. She was flushed red, her eyes were very wide open and queer, her upper lip lifted away from her two white, front teeth with a curious, almost rabbit look.

A little stout man in a black overcoat and a bowler hat came pottering across the yard. He had a pink face and a white beard and smallish, pale-blue eyes. He was not very old, but nervy, and he walked with little short steps.

'What do you think, father?' said Banford. 'Don't you think it might hit the shed in falling?'

'Shed, no!' said the old man. 'Can't hit the shed. Might as well say the fence.'

'The fence doesn't matter,' said March, in her high voice.

'Wrong as usual, am I!' said Banford, wiping her straying hair from her eyes.

The tree stood as it were on one spelch of itself, leaning, and creaking in the wind. It grew on the bank of a little dry ditch between the two meadows. On the top of the bank straggled one fence, running to the bushes up-hill. Several trees clustered there in the corner of the field near the shed and near the gate which led into the yard. Towards this gate, horizontal across the weary meadows, came the grassy, rutted approach from the high road. There trailed another rickety fence, long split poles joining the short, thick, wide-apart uprights. The three people stood at the back of the tree, in the corner of the shed meadow, just above the yard gate. The house, with its two gables and its porch, stood tidy in a little grassed garden across the yard. A little, stout, rosy-faced woman in a little red woollen shoulder shawl had come and taken her stand in the porch.

'Isn't it down yet?' she cried, in a high little voice.

'Just thinking about it,' called her husband. His tone towards the two girls was always rather mocking and satirical. March did not want to go on with her hitting while he was there. As for him, he wouldn't lift a stick from the ground if he could help it, complaining, like his daughter, of rheumatics in his shoulder. So the three stood there a moment silent in the cold afternoon, in the bottom corner near the yard.

They heard the far-off taps of a gate, and craned to look. Away across, on the green horizontal approach, a figure was just swinging on to a bicycle again, and lurching up and down over the grass, approaching.

'Why, it's one of our boys - it's Jack,' said the old man.

'Can't be,' said Banford.

March craned her head to look. She alone recognized the khaki figure. She flushed, but said nothing.

'No, it isn't Jack, I don't think,' said the old man, staring with little round blue eyes under his white lashes.

In another moment the bicycle lurched into sight, and the rider dropped off at the gate. It was Henry, his face wet and red and spotted with mud. He was altogether a muddy sight.

'Oh!' cried Banford, as if afraid. 'Why, it's Henry!'

'What?' muttered the old man. He had a thick, rapid, muttering way of speaking, and was slightly deaf. 'What? What? Who is it? Who is it, do you say? That young fellow? That young fellow of Nellie's? Oh! Oh!' And the satiric smile came on his pink face and white eyelashes.

Henry, pushing the wet hair off his steaming brow, had caught sight of them and heard what the old man said. His hot, young face seemed to flame in the cold light.

'Oh, are you all there!' he said, giving his sudden, puppy's little laugh. He was so hot and dazed with cycling he hardly knew where he was. He leaned the bicycle against the fence and climbed over into the corner on to the bank, without going into the yard.

'Well, I must say, we weren't expecting YOU,' said Banford laconically.

'No, I suppose not,' said he, looking at March.

She stood aside, slack, with one knee drooped and the axe resting its head loosely on the ground. Her eyes were wide and vacant, and her upper lip lifted from her teeth in that helpless, fascinated rabbit look. The moment she saw his glowing, red face it was all over with her. She was as helpless as if she had been bound. The moment she saw the way his head seemed to reach forward.

'Well, who is it? Who is it, anyway?' asked the smiling, satiric old man in his muttering voice.

'Why, Mr Grenfel, whom you've heard us tell about, father,' said Banford coldly.

'Heard you tell about, I should think so. Heard of nothing else practically,' muttered the elderly man, with his queer little jeering smile on his face. 'How do you do,' he added, suddenly reaching out his hand to Henry.

The boy shook hands just as startled. Then the two men fell apart.

'Cycled over from Salisbury Plain, have you?' asked the old man.

'Yes.'

'Hm! Longish ride. How long d'it take you, eh? Some time, eh? Several hours, I suppose.'

'About four.'

'Eh? Four! Yes, I should have thought so. When are you going back, then?'

'I've got till tomorrow evening.'

'Till tomorrow evening, eh? Yes. Hm! Girls weren't expecting you, were they?'

And the old man turned his pale-blue, round little eyes under their white lashes mockingly towards the girls. Henry also looked round. He had become a little awkward. He looked at March, who was still staring away into the distance as if to see where the cattle were. Her hand was on the pommel of the axe, whose head rested loosely on the ground.

'What were you doing there?' he asked in his soft, courteous voice. 'Cutting a tree down?'

March seemed not to hear, as if in a trance.

'Yes,' said Banford. 'We've been at it for over a week.'

'Oh! And have you done it all by yourselves then?'

'Nellie's done it all, I've done nothing,' said Banford.

'Really! You must have worked quite hard,' he said, addressing himself in a curious gentle tone direct to March. She did not answer, but remained half averted staring away towards the woods above as if in a trance.

'NELLIE!' cried Banford sharply. 'Can't you answer?'

'What - me?' cried March, starting round and looking from one to the other. 'Did anyone speak to me?'

'Dreaming!' muttered the old man, turning aside to smile. 'Must be in love, eh, dreaming in the daytime!'

'Did you say anything to me?' said March, looking at the boy as from a strange distance, her eyes wide and doubtful, her face delicately flushed.

'I said you must have worked hard at the tree,' he replied courteously.

'Oh, that! Bit by bit. I thought it would have come down by now.'

125

'I'm thankful it hasn't come down in the night, to frighten us to death,' said Banford.

'Let me just finish it for you, shall I?' said the boy.

March slanted the axe-shaft in his direction.

'Would you like to?' she said.

'Yes, if you wish it,' he said.

'Oh, I'm thankful when the thing's down, that's all,' she replied, nonchalant.

'Which way is it going to fall?' said Banford. 'Will it hit the shed?'

'No, it won't hit the shed,' he said. 'I should think it will fall there - quite clear. Though it might give a twist and catch the fence.'

'Catch the fence!' cried the old man. 'What, catch the fence! When it's leaning at that angle? Why, it's farther off than the shed. It won't catch the fence.'

'No,' said Henry, 'I don't suppose it will. It has plenty of room to fall quite clear, and I suppose it will fall clear.'

'Won't tumble backwards on top of US, will it?' asked the old man, sarcastic.

'No, it won't do that,' said Henry, taking off his short overcoat and his tunic. 'Ducks! Ducks! Go back!'

A line of four brown-speckled ducks led by a brown-and-green drake were stemming away downhill from the upper meadow, coming like boats running on a ruffled sea, cockling their way top speed downwards towards the fence and towards the little group of people, and cackling as excitedly as if they brought news of the Spanish Armada.

'Silly things! Silly things!' cried Banford, going forward to turn them off. But they came eagerly towards her, opening their yellow-green beaks and quacking as if they were so excited to say something.

'There's no food. There's nothing here. You must wait a bit,' said Banford to them. 'Go away. Go away. Go round to the yard.'

They didn't go, so she climbed the fence to swerve them round under the gate and into the yard. So off they waggled in an excited string once more, wagging their rumps like the stems of little gondolas, ducking under the bar of the gate. Banford stood on the top of the bank, just over the fence, looking down on the other three.

Henry looked up at her, and met her queer, round-pupilled, weak eyes staring behind her spectacles. He was perfectly still. He looked away, up at the weak, leaning tree. And as he looked into the sky, like a huntsman who is watching a flying bird, he thought to himself: 'If the tree falls in just such a way, and spins just so much as it falls, then the branch there will strike her exactly as she stands on top of that bank.'

He looked at her again. She was wiping the hair from her brow again, with that perpetual gesture. In his heart he had decided her death. A terrible still force seemed in him, and a power that was just his. If he turned even a hair's breadth in the wrong direction, he would lose the power.

'Mind yourself, Miss Banford,' he said. And his heart held perfectly still, in the terrible pure will that she should not move.

'Who, me, mind myself?' she cried, her father's jeering tone in her voice. 'Why, do you think you might hit me with the axe?'

'No, it's just possible the tree might, though,' he answered soberly. But the tone of his voice seemed to her to imply that he was only being falsely solicitous, and trying to make her move because it was his will to move her.

'Absolutely impossible,' she said.

He heard her. But he held himself icy still, lest he should lose his power.

'No, it's just possible. You'd better come down this way.'

'Oh, all right. Let us see some crack Canadian tree-felling,' she retorted.

'Ready, then,' he said, taking the axe, looking round to see he was clear.

There was a moment of pure, motionless suspense, when the world seemed to stand still. Then suddenly his form seemed to flash up enormously tall and fearful, he gave two swift, flashing blows, in immediate succession, the tree was severed, turning slowly, spinning strangely in the air and coming down like a sudden darkness on the earth. No one saw what was happening except himself. No one heard the strange little cry which the Banford gave as the dark end of the bough swooped down, down on her. No one saw her crouch a little and receive the blow on the back of the neck. No one saw her flung outwards and laid, a little twitching heap, at the foot of the fence. No one except the boy. And he watched with intense bright eyes, as he would watch a wild goose he had shot. Was it winged or dead? Dead!

Immediately he gave a loud cry. Immediately March gave a wild shriek that went far, far down the afternoon. And the father started a strange bellowing sound.

The boy leapt the fence and ran to the fringe. The back of the neck and head was a mass of blood, of horror. He turned it over. The body was quivering with little convulsions. But she was dead really. He knew it, that it was so. He knew it in his soul and his blood. The inner necessity of his life was fulfilling itself, it was he who was to live. The thorn was drawn out of his bowels. So he put her down gently. She was dead.

He stood up. March was standing there petrified and absolutely motionless. Her face was dead white, her eyes big black pools. The old man was scrambling horribly over the fence.

'I'm afraid it's killed her,' said the boy.

The old man was making curious, blubbering noises as he huddled over the fence. 'What!' cried March, starting electric.

'Yes, I'm afraid,' repeated the boy.

March was coming forward. The boy was over the fence before she reached it.

'What do you say, killed her?' she asked in a sharp voice.

'I'm afraid so,' he answered softly.

She went still whiter, fearful. The two stood facing one another. Her black eyes gazed on him with the last look of resistance. And then in a last agonized failure she began to grizzle, to cry in a shivery little fashion of a child that doesn't want to cry, but which is beaten from within, and gives that little first shudder of sobbing which is not yet weeping, dry and fearful.

He had won. She stood there absolutely helpless, shuddering her dry sobs and her mouth trembling rapidly. And then, as in a child, with a little crash came the tears and the blind agony of sightless weeping. She sank down on the grass, and sat there with her hands on her breast and her face lifted in sightless, convulsed weeping. He stood above her, looking down on her, mute, pale, and everlasting seeming. He never moved, but looked down on her. And among all the torture of the scene, the torture of his own heart and bowels, he was glad, he had won.

After a long time he stooped to her and took her hands.

'Don't cry,' he said softly. 'Don't cry.'

She looked up at him with tears running from her eyes, a senseless look of helplessness and submission. So she gazed on him as if sightless, yet looking up to him. She would never leave him again. He had won her. And he knew it and was glad, because he wanted her for his life. His life must have her. And now he had won her. It was what his life must have.

But if he had won her, he had not yet got her. They were married at Christmas as he had planned, and he got again ten days' leave. They went to Cornwall, to his own village, on the sea. He realized that it was awful for her to be at the farm any more.

But though she belonged to him, though she lived in his shadow, as if she could not be away from him, she was not happy. She did not want to leave him: and yet she did not feel free with him. Everything round her seemed to watch her, seemed to press on her. He had won her, he had her with him, she was his wife. And she - she belonged to him, she knew it. But she was not glad. And he was still foiled. He realized that though he was married to her and possessed her in every possible way, apparently, and though she WANTED him to possess her, she wanted it, she wanted nothing else, now, still he did not quite succeed.

Something was missing. Instead of her soul swaying with new life, it seemed to droop, to bleed, as if it were wounded. She would sit for a long time with her hand in his, looking away at the sea. And in her dark, vacant eyes was a sort of wound, and her face looked a little peaked. If he spoke to her, she would turn to him with a faint new smile, the strange, quivering little smile of a woman who has died in the old way of love, and can't quite rise to the new way. She still felt she ought to DO something, to strain herself in some direction. And there was nothing to do, and no direction in which to strain herself. And she could not quite accept the submergence which his new love put upon her. If she was in love, she ought to EXERT herself, in some way, loving. She felt the weary need of our day to EXERT herself in love. But she knew that in fact she must no more exert herself in love. He would not have the love which exerted itself towards him. It made his brow go black. No, he wouldn't let her exert her love towards him. No, she had to be passive, to acquiesce, and to be submerged under the surface of love. She had to be like the seaweeds she saw as she peered down from the boat, swaying forever delicately under water, with all their delicate fibrils put tenderly out upon the flood, sensitive, utterly sensitive and receptive within the shadowy sea, and never, never rising and looking forth above water while they lived. Never. Never looking forth from the water until they died, only then washing, corpses, upon the surface. But while they lived, always submerged, always beneath the wave. Beneath the wave they might have powerful roots, stronger than iron; they might be tenacious and dangerous in their soft waving within the flood. Beneath the water they might be stronger, more indestructible than resistant oak trees are on land. But it was always under-water, always under-water. And she, being a woman, must be like that.

And she had been so used to the very opposite. She had had to take all the thought for love and for life, and all the responsibility. Day after day she had been responsible for the coming day, for the coming year: for her dear Jill's health and happiness and well-being. Verily, in her own small way, she had felt herself responsible for the well-being of the world. And this had been her great stimulant, this grand feeling that, in her own small sphere, she was responsible for the well-being of the world.

And she had failed. She knew that, even in her small way, she had failed. She had failed to satisfy her own feeling of responsibility. It was so difficult. It seemed so grand and easy at first. And the more you tried, the more difficult it became. It had seemed so easy to make one beloved creature happy. And the more you tried, the worse the failure. It was terrible. She had been all her life reaching, reaching, and what she reached for seemed so near, until she had stretched to her utmost limit. And then it was always beyond her.

Always beyond her, vaguely, unrealizably beyond her, and she was left with nothingness at last. The life she reached for, the happiness she reached for, the well-being she reached for all slipped back, became unreal, the farther she stretched her hand. She wanted some goal, some finality - and there was none. Always this ghastly reaching, reaching, striving for something that might be just beyond. Even to make Jill happy. She was glad Jill was dead. For she had realized that she could never make her happy. Jill would always be fretting herself thinner and thinner, weaker and weaker. Her pains grew worse instead of less. It would be so for ever. She was glad she was dead.

And if Jill had married a man it would have been just the same. The woman striving, striving to make the man happy, striving within her own limits for the well-being of her world. And always achieving failure. Little, foolish successes in money or in ambition. But at the very point where she most wanted success, in the anguished effort to make some one beloved human being happy and perfect, there the failure was almost catastrophic. You wanted to make your beloved happy, and his happiness seemed always achievable. If only you did just this, that, and the other. And you did this, that, and the other, in all good faith, and every time the failure became a little more ghastly. You could love yourself to ribbons and strive and strain yourself to the bone, and things would go from bad to worse, bad to worse, as far as happiness went. The awful mistake of happiness.

Poor March, in her good-will and her responsibility, she had strained herself till it seemed to her that the whole of life and everything was only a horrible abyss of nothingness. The more you reached after the fatal flower of happiness, which trembles so blue and lovely in a crevice just beyond your grasp, the more fearfully you became aware of the ghastly and awful gulf of the precipice below you, into which you will inevitably plunge, as into the bottomless pit, if you reach any farther. You pluck flower after flower - it is never THE flower. The flower itself - its calyx is a horrible gulf, it is the bottomless pit.

That is the whole history of the search for happiness, whether it be your own or somebody else's that you want to win. It ends, and it always ends, in the ghastly sense of the bottomless nothingness into which you will inevitably fall if you strain any farther.

And women? - what goal can any woman conceive, except happiness? Just happiness for herself and the whole world. That, and nothing else. And so, she assumes the responsibility and sets off towards her goal. She can see it there, at the foot of the rainbow. Or she can see it a little way beyond, in the blue distance. Not far, not far.

But the end of the rainbow is a bottomless gulf down which you can fall forever without arriving, and the blue distance is a void pit which can swallow you and all your efforts into its emptiness, and still be no emptier. You and all your efforts. So, the illusion of attainable happiness!

Poor March, she had set off so wonderfully towards the blue goal. And the farther and farther she had gone, the more fearful had become the realization of emptiness. An agony, an insanity at last.

She was glad it was over. She was glad to sit on the shore and look westwards over the sea, and know the great strain had ended. She would never strain for love and happiness any more. And Jill was safely dead. Poor Jill, poor Jill. It must be sweet to be dead.

For her own part, death was not her destiny. She would have to leave her destiny to the boy. But then, the boy. He wanted more than that. He wanted her to give herself without defences, to sink and become submerged in him. And she - she wanted to sit still, like a woman on the last milestone, and watch. She wanted to see, to know, to understand. She wanted to be alone: with him at her side.

And he! He did not want her to watch any more, to see any more, to understand any more. He wanted to veil her woman's spirit, as Orientals veil the woman's face. He wanted her to commit herself to him, and to put her independent spirit to sleep. He wanted to take away from her all her effort, all that seemed her very raison d'etre. He wanted to make her submit, yield, blindly pass away out of all her strenuous consciousness. He wanted to take away her consciousness, and make her just his woman. Just his woman.

And she was so tired, so tired, like a child that wants to go to sleep, but which fights against sleep as if sleep were death. She seemed to stretch her eyes wider in the obstinate effort and tension of keeping awake. She WOULD keep awake. She WOULD know. She WOULD consider and judge and decide. She would have the reins of her own life between her own hands. She WOULD be an independent woman to the last. But she was so tired, so tired of everything. And sleep seemed near. And there was such rest in the boy.

Yet there, sitting in a niche of the high, wild, cliffs of West Cornwall, looking over the westward sea, she stretched her eyes wider and wider. Away to the West, Canada, America. She WOULD know and she WOULD see what was ahead. And the boy, sitting beside her, staring down at the gulls, had a cloud between his brows and the strain of discontent in his eyes. He wanted her asleep, at peace in him. He wanted her at peace asleep in him. And THERE she was, dying with the strain of her own wakefulness. Yet she would not sleep: no, never. Sometimes he thought bitterly that he ought to have left her. He ought never to have killed Banford. He should have left Banford and March to kill one another.

But that was only impatience: and he knew it. He was waiting, waiting to go West. He was aching almost in torment to leave England, to go West, to take March away. To leave this shore! He believed that as they crossed the seas, as they left this England which he so hated, because in some way it seemed to have stung him with poison, she would go to sleep. She would close her eyes at last and give in to him.

And then he would have her, and he would have his own life at last. He chafed, feeling he hadn't got his own life. He would never have it till she yielded and slept in him. Then he would have all his own life as a young man and a male, and she would have all her own life as a woman and a female. There would be no more of this awful straining. She would not be a man any more, an independent woman with a man's responsibility. Nay, even the responsibility for her own soul she would have to commit to him. He knew it was so, and obstinately held out against her, waiting for the surrender.

'You'll feel better when once we get over the seas to Canada over there,' he said to her as they sat among the rocks on the cliff.

She looked away to the sea's horizon, as if it were not real. Then she looked round at him, with the strained, strange look of a child that is struggling against sleep.

'Shall I?' she said.

'Yes,' he answered quietly.

And her eyelids dropped with the slow motion, sleep weighing them unconscious. But she pulled them open again to say:

'Yes, I may. I can't tell. I can't tell what it will be like over there.'

'If only we could go soon!' he said, with pain in his voice.

- The End -

www.ingramcontent.com/pod-product-compliance
Lightning Source LLC
Chambersburg PA
CBHW030537130626
46552CB00006B/2307